Hard To Serve

Also From Laura Kaye

The Raven Riders Series
Ride Hard
Ride Rough

The Hard Ink Series:
Hard As It Gets
Hard As You Can
Hard to Hold On To
Hard to Come By
Hard to Be Good
Hard to Let Go
Hard Ever After
Hard As Steel
Hard Ever After
Hard To Serve

The Hearts in Darkness Duet
Hearts In Darkness
Love In The Light

The Heroes Series
Her Forbidden Hero
One Night With A Hero

Hard To Serve

A HARD INK NOVELLA

By Laura Kaye

1001 Dark Nights

EVIL EYE
CONCEPTS

HARD TO SERVE
A HARD INK NOVELLA
BY LAURA KAYE

1001 Dark Nights
Copyright 2016 Laura Kaye
ISBN: 978-1-942299-27-1

Foreword: Copyright 2014 M. J. Rose
Published by Evil Eye Concepts, Incorporated

Acknowledgments from the Author

Sometimes, you get to do really fun things with super cool people – and that's totally the case with my 1001 Dark Nights books. The whole Dark Nights family, from Liz and M.J. to Jillian to all the other authors, is simply fantastic to work with, and I will remain forever grateful to Liz Berry for bringing me into the fold. And I have to thank both Liz and Jillian for their habit of texting me their reactions when they read my work – it's the most fun an author can have with their phone!

Next, I need to thank my best friend and fellow author Lea Nolan for helping me brainstorm parts of the book and for cheerleading me through! How lucky am I that get to work with my bestie every day?

Thanks, as always, to my husband and daughter for supporting me and giving me the time that it takes to finish a book. I'm so fortunate to have the love and support of my family, and I can't thank them enough.

Finally, thank you to my Heroes for all your help and support, to my Reader Girls for squeeing over early excerpts from this book, and to all the readers of my books—you take my characters into your hearts and let them tell their stories over and over again, and for that, I thank you from the bottom of my heart. ~LK

To Liz~

The gardener of ideas
The cultivator of magic
The builder of castles in the air
You build me and everyone around you up. And I'm so grateful to know
you.

Sign up for the 1001 Dark Nights Newsletter
and be entered to win a Tiffany Key necklace.

There's a contest every month!

Go to www.1001DarkNights.com to subscribe.

As a bonus, all subscribers will receive a free
1001 Dark Nights story
The First Night
by Lexi Blake & M.J. Rose

One Thousand and One Dark Nights

Once upon a time, in the future…

*I was a student fascinated with stories and learning.
I studied philosophy, poetry, history, the occult, and
the art and science of love and magic. I had a vast
library at my father's home and collected thousands
of volumes of fantastic tales.*

*I learned all about ancient races and bygone
times. About myths and legends and dreams of all
people through the millennium. And the more I read
the stronger my imagination grew until I discovered
that I was able to travel into the stories... to actually
become part of them.*

*I wish I could say that I listened to my teacher
and respected my gift, as I ought to have. If I had, I
would not be telling you this tale now.
But I was foolhardy and confused, showing off
with bravery.*

*One afternoon, curious about the myth of the
Arabian Nights, I traveled back to ancient Persia to
see for myself if it was true that every day Shahryar
(Persian: شهريار, "king") married a new virgin, and then
sent yesterday's wife to be beheaded. It was written
and I had read, that by the time he met Scheherazade,
the vizier's daughter, he'd killed one thousand
women.*

*Something went wrong with my efforts. I arrived
in the midst of the story and somehow exchanged
places with Scheherazade — a phenomena that had
never occurred before and that still to this day, I
cannot explain.*

*Now I am trapped in that ancient past. I have
taken on Scheherazade's life and the only way I can
protect myself and stay alive is to do what she did to
protect herself and stay alive.*

*Every night the King calls for me and listens as I spin tales.
And when the evening ends and dawn breaks, I stop at a
point that leaves him breathless and yearning for more.
And so the King spares my life for one more day, so that
he might hear the rest of my dark tale.*

*As soon as I finish a story... I begin a new
one... like the one that you, dear reader, have before
you now.*

"I went to the woods because I wished to live deliberately, to front only the essential facts of life, and see if I could not learn what it had to teach, and not, when I came to die, discover that I had not lived. I did not wish to live what was not life, living is so dear; nor did I wish to practise resignation, unless it was quite necessary. I wanted to live deep and suck out all the marrow of life."

~Henry David Thoreau

Chapter 1

"You're on restricted duty, pending medical clearance, Detective Vance," Captain Mike Burkett said, his voice unusually formal as his gaze lifted from the file of paperwork. Probably because of the suit from internal affairs sitting beside him. Why the hell was that guy here for Vance's evaluation to return to duty anyway?

Detective Kyler Vance. That's who he was. Who he'd always been. Who he needed to get back to being. He'd had enough time off and on his own to last for a lifetime.

Kyler eyeballed the IA investigator and his gut tightened with suspicion. But he boxed that shit up tight even as his hands fisted against his thighs under the beat-up wooden table in the meeting room at the Baltimore Police Department's headquarters. "Cap, it's been three months," he said, working to keep his temper in check. Three months since he'd been shot in the shoulder in the line of duty. Three months since that GSW had left him with nerve damage that affected the strength and dexterity of his right arm and hand. "I'm fine. I can do the job."

His captain gave him a pointed look full of truth and regret. "You still can't meet the target-shooting qualifications. So you're riding a desk. For now."

For now. Meaning, at some point, Kyler might be allowed to return to duty. *Or* he might not even be allowed behind that desk. Everyone wearing the uniform had to meet certain performance qualifications and standards, no matter what job they performed. Which was why Kyler had been one hundred percent committed to his physical therapy since a shooting spree erupted at a funeral attended by a bunch of his friends, killing a couple of bad guys and wounding more than a few good ones, himself included. But it had all been worth it to nail the scumbags responsible for murdering his godfather, Miguel Olivero, who had been his father's partner on the force back in the day. "You know I'm working on it. I'm stronger every day."

Burkett nodded and released a weary breath. All at once, the lines on the older man's weathered face betrayed not just his age but the stress he was under. Serving and protecting was an honor, but it was also a job that inflicted all kinds of wear and tear. "I know. And if there was something I could do—"

"But there isn't," the IA guy said. Detective Niall Foster, his badge read. Kyler had seen him around from time to time, but he didn't know him much more than that. Cops didn't make friends with IA investigators. "I'll tell you what Captain Burkett hasn't yet said. You're lucky to be on restricted duty and not administrative leave."

"Why the hell would I be on administrative leave?" Anger rolled through Kyler at the other man's monotone voice and blank face, as if he wasn't fucking with the only career Kyler Vance had ever wanted. Career, hell. Being a cop was his whole damn life. Just like it'd been for his father, uncle, and grandfather before him.

Foster flipped open the file in front of him and skimmed his finger over the writing. "You're no doubt aware that Commissioner Breslin has launched an investigation into corruption and conspiracy within the department, particularly as it relates to the city's heroin trade. Your name has come to the attention of the investigation as a person of interest, and—"

"Wait a goddamned minute," Kyler said, launching to his feet and driving his finger into the worn tabletop. He couldn't deny that he'd bent some rules in the weeks before his injury, but he'd done it in the name of uncovering that corruption—and nailing those responsible for Miguel's death, both inside and outside BPD. Kyler supported the new commissioner's goals to restore the integrity of the department, even if the guy was a hardassed, stubborn, my-way-or-the-highway son of a bitch. At least, that's the impression all the guys had of him—Kyler hadn't yet had the pleasure. "I'm not dirty, and I'd like the person who accused me of being otherwise to say it to my fucking face."

"Sit down, please, Detective Vance," Foster said, gesturing to the chair behind him. Kyler sat reluctantly, but his muscles remained as tense as if he were expecting to be jumped. He certainly felt like he was being ambushed here. He glared at Burkett, who at least had the decency to look abashed. "No one has accused you. You're not currently a suspect. But you are a person of interest in the investigation. Which, together with the fact that your physical limitations have placed you on restricted duty, is why you aren't being put on administrative leave."

The phrase "physical limitations" was like a punch to the gut. Yeah, his shoulder and arm hurt sometimes—when steel pierced flesh you expected that shit to happen. But he could handle it, and he'd been working his ass off and was capable of ninety-nine percent of daily life functioning again. What he hadn't yet mastered was superfine motor skills, of the kind that made you a reliably deadly accurate shot, for example. What if those skills never returned?

"So what the hell does it mean then? What will it take for the investigation to be done being interested in me?" Kyler asked, his hackles still way up.

"Time," Foster said on a sigh, as if he were bored.

Prick.

"If you're clean, the investigation will clear you and you have nothing to worry about." As if that settled the matter, the man scooped up his paperwork and rose. "Commissioner Breslin wants to restore the department's good name in this city and within the law enforcement community. Surely you can understand that. Support him in this mission, stay out of trouble and do your duty, and this will resolve itself in due course." Foster looked to his side and nodded. "Captain Burkett."

"Foster," his captain said as the IA guy turned and walked out the door, the stick firmly planted up his ass.

Kyler's gaze cut to Burkett. "This is bullshit."

"It is," Burkett said, sitting forward in his chair as if he were about to share a secret. "But it's also reality. And the more you stay on Breslin's good side, the easier this will go and the faster it will disappear. Understand me?"

Stay on the commissioner's good side. A long moment, then Kyler gave a single, tight nod. Since he hadn't done anything wrong, that shouldn't be all that fucking hard.

"Roger that." Kyler rose when his captain did.

"Take care of yourself," Burkett said, extending his hand. They shook, and then Kyler found himself alone in the room.

Take care of himself. Fine. He could do that. What he needed after this shit show was to blow off some fucking steam. It had been months—well, before getting shot—since he'd last played. It was time.

Which meant that what he needed was Blasphemy.

* * * *

Standing in the middle of her gleaming, modern gallery, the new exhibit installed and ready for Friday night's opening, Mia Breslin couldn't help but feel proud of herself and excited for her life to be coming together exactly the way she'd always hoped. Fantastic job in a field that was her passion—art. That she got paid good money to work at something she loved was amazing. That her work allowed her to network with prominent artists, collectors, and buyers while still working on her own projects was an incredible privilege.

All of which amplified the one area of discontent and hollowness in Mia's life—that she had no one to share it with. More than that, finding the *right* someone seemed like it just might be impossible.

Why'd you have to go and have such a difficult kink? her best friend Daniella would say.

Because nothing else turned her on like being dominated. And nothing else got her off like submitting.

Problem was, finding a man who wasn't just a Dominant but who wore that authority naturally, like a second skin, like it was the air he breathed, like it was in his blood and he knew no other way? *That* apparently was hard as hell. And her body seemed to know the difference—on sight—between someone playing at dominating and someone who was the real thing.

Sighing, Mia crossed the wide gallery located in a rehabbed warehouse space in an up-and-coming area of Baltimore, her heels clicking against the shining hardwoods. Sitting at her desk, she woke up her computer screen and logged into her private e-mail—the one out of which she ran all of her lifestyle communications. And then she opened the message she'd been sitting on for nearly two weeks—a coveted and rare invitation to Baltimore's most exclusive BDSM club, Blasphemy.

Before she'd even moved to Baltimore four months before, Mia had already looked into the community in Baltimore, hoping she'd find more of one than there'd been in the smaller college towns where she'd done her graduate work and had her first job. When she'd learned about Blasphemy through message boards to which she belonged, she'd been ecstatic and immediately started the lengthy application and clearance process. But there was a difference between the idea of something and the reality. Before Baltimore, she'd only been to private play parties and one lame club that'd left a lot to be desired where cleanliness and safety were concerned.

But Blasphemy was different. That's what everyone said.

"I need this," she whispered to herself. She needed the incredible release of submission, and she needed someone strong enough to truly give it to her. Again and again and again.

Before she let herself overthink it, she printed out the ticket that would gain her admittance and a two-week, discounted probationary membership. And discounted was perfect, because as good as her job paid—especially for something in the art world—her student loans ate up a lot of her monthly income. And it wasn't like she could ask her father for money to belong to a BDSM club. He'd probably have a heart attack, right after he sent in a SWAT team to close the place down.

An hour later, she was home, showered, and had gone through all the play clothes she kept in a trunk at the back of her closet. Going to her knees with a wad of latex in her lap, Mia took a deep breath and sent out an SOS in the form of a text to her best friend, Daniella, who'd recently landed a new job in DC—not as close as Mia would've liked but close enough to still see one another and stay in each other's lives.

Kinda want to check out that club I told you about but I'm freaking out.

Mia's phone rang within twenty seconds. Laughing, she answered. "Hi."

"Stop freaking out," Daniella said by way of greeting.

"Why, thank you for that excellent advice," Mia said, already feeling better just hearing Dani's voice.

"Come on, you know you messaged me to get the tough love," Dani said, humor plain in her tone. "Why are you freaking out?"

"I can't figure out what to wear." Mia sorted through the pile on the floor. "And I'm afraid I won't find anyone. *And* I'm also afraid I might find someone and he won't want me." Or, rather, he won't want a cop's daughter. In her experience, more than a few Doms got freaked out at the idea of tying up and spanking a police officer's daughter. And now her dad wasn't just *any* policeman, either. As of two months ago, he was the city's new commissioner of police.

"Okay, I got this," Dani said. "On clothes, go with the sheer white lace top over that sheer black bra you have, and wear it with that little latex skirt with the asymmetrical hem and those black ankle boots. Put your hair in a ponytail. Boom. Done."

Mia found the pieces Dani suggested. "That is a good outfit," she admitted. Even though it really showed off how big her boobs and hips were. Her body was the shape of an hourglass on steroids—wide on the top and bottom and narrow in the middle.

"I know, right? I'm, like, the submissive whisperer," she said, making herself laugh. "And on the bigger, existential fears, fuck 'em. We might all die tomorrow. You gotta suck all the marrow out of life. That's what Walt Whitman said."

Chuckling, Mia nodded to herself. "I think that was Thoreau."

"Same difference," Dani said.

"We might all die tomorrow, huh?" Mia mused, her mind spinning on the Thoreau quote. She definitely didn't want to die without really having lived. And, for her, that meant finding a long-term Dom and having a fulfilling BDSM relationship. Anything else would be resignation, and even though she was only twenty-seven, the idea of that terrified her. The last thing she wanted was to end up like her parents—divorced and full of regrets over the time they'd spent together. "That's super cheerful, you know."

"Heh. Exactly," Dani said. "I excel at putting things into perspective."

Dani's words and snarky attitude had done exactly what Mia had hoped—they'd bolstered her resolve. She rose to her feet, the outfit Dani recommended in hand. "You also excel at being my friend."

"I really am quite awesome."

Mia barked out a laugh. "You are. Okay, thank you. I'm doing this."

"Of course you are. I want a full report tomorrow," Dani said, her voice stern.

"Duly noted." Smiling, Mia threw the clothing on her bed. "See you Friday?"

"Wouldn't miss your big opening for the world, my friend. Now go kick some Dominant ass."

"Uh, it's kind of the other way around." Mia chuckled at her friend's awesome ridiculousness as they hung up.

But now she almost felt like she could do just that. Or, at least, drive some Dominant ass totally crazy with lust. Thoughts of exactly what that might involve lanced heat through her whole body.

Within a half an hour, she was dressed and catching a cab across town, a long trench coat covering the indecency of her outfit until she got inside the club.

"Here we are," the cab driver called over his shoulder as he pulled to the curb.

As she paid, Mia peered out the window. The neighborhood was heavy on old warehouses and light on actual residences. And her destination was no exception. The large brick building ran the whole length of the block. Lights illuminated a set of double doors and a sign that read, "Club Diablo." A line formed at the dance club's door and snaked into the dimness.

"Thank you," she said to the cabby as she got out.

Giving her ticket another once-over, she approached the bouncer, but before she'd even gotten close enough to hand it to him, he spotted it and directed her inside the foyer and through a door off to one side. The door led her down a long hallway that must've run along the mainstream club, judging by the way the bass beat echoed like a heartbeat inside the narrow space, but then finally sent her back outdoors again into the well-lit courtyard of what appeared to be a huge, old church. Outside the arched doors of what had once been the church's front stood another mountain of a man in an exquisitely cut black suit. He pointed her in the direction of a ramp that sloped down and around the outside of the long, rectangular nave to another set of doors and a third bouncer, again wearing a black-on-black suit.

A shiver ran over Mia's skin because she was here, and she was really doing this. She held out her ticket, which the bouncer scanned with a device in his hand. Then he opened the door, his voice deep and inviting as he said, "Welcome to Blasphemy. Have a good night."

Chapter 2

Kyler sat in the control room at Blasphemy, his gaze half on the monitors as he shot the shit with Isaac Marten, another of the club's twelve Masters—experienced Dominants who possessed an ownership stake in Blasphemy and took turns running and monitoring the club. Kyler had bought his share of the business with a chunk of his own savings and the money his grandfather had left him, and now his investment paid him back in spades.

This wasn't one of Kyler's nights to be on, but many of them dropped in to hang out or play outside of their scheduled shifts, so no one thought anything odd about Kyler being there on a random Wednesday. Unlike on the force, here at Blasphemy Kyler wasn't *the one who was hurt* or *the one on medical leave* or, now, *the one under investigation*. Here, he was just Master Kyler, and none of the other men tiptoed around him like they were starting to do in the department. Here, the only ones who did the tiptoeing around him were the subs. As it should be. The thought almost eked a smile out of him.

"You heading out onto the floor?" Isaac asked, turning dark eyes toward Kyler. In his day job, Isaac ran a security business—high-tech gadgets were his thing, a principle that extended in interesting and creative ways into his scenes.

Shrugging, Kyler scrubbed his hands through his brown hair. Longer than he usually let it get. "At some point." While he'd fulfilled most of his duty rotations as one of the Masters here, he hadn't done any scenes since before getting shot. Early on, that'd been because he'd been in too much pain. Later, it'd been because even as he healed, his arm was too weak and had too little control to feel confident that he could adequately wield a paddle or support a woman's weight. Now, fucking target-shooting qualifications aside, he was feeling more his usual self, his body almost back to one hundred percent.

Next to one of the keyboards, Isaac's cell beeped an incoming text. The man picked it up, smiled, and replied.

"How's Willow?" Kyler asked, recognizing the happy expression on Isaac's dark brown face.

Isaac nodded, still wearing a smile. "She's good. She keeps saying she's as big as a house, but there's nothing like seeing your woman's belly grow with your child."

"Two more months?" Kyler asked, the reverence of the other man's tone getting under his skin, just a little. Not because he wanted Willow for himself, but because at thirty-five, Kyler already knew he'd never have any of what Isaac and Willow had. He couldn't. Being married hadn't worked out well for either his father or grandfather. The force was a jealous fucking mistress. It put a shit-ton of stress on a spouse's shoulders and therefore on the relationship itself. He'd rather forego the heartache and stick with the eventual aloneness that seemed the curse of all the Vance men.

That was why Kyler had his rules. Never get attached. Share and seek out only that personal information needed to determine a sub's needs, interests, and limits. Stop playing with a submissive showing signs of attachment. Never play outside the club. Never take a submissive home.

"Yup. It's gonna be interesting, adapting all this to the reality of a child," Isaac said, waving a hand to indicate the club, the lifestyle, maybe even life itself.

"No doubt," Kyler said. "You'll manage, though."

"Always do," Isaac said, scrubbing a hand over his close-cropped black hair. Suddenly, he sat forward and zoomed one of the cameras in on the registration area. "Looks like we got a new subbie."

Kyler's gaze followed Isaac's to the image of a woman sitting bolt upright on the edge of the chair in front of the registration desk, her ankles crossed, her hands folded in her lap. Long, straight, dark brown hair hung all the way down her back from a high ponytail. Master Griffin was no doubt walking her through the rules and procedures, verifying her hard and soft limits, and preparing the wrist cuffs that all the unattached submissives wore to indicate what kind of play in which they were or were not willing to engage.

Heat shot through Kyler's blood in anticipation of seeing what color kink ribbons would adorn her cuffs, heat that surged as Griffin added more and more colors to those cuffs. Kyler also liked what he didn't see. No white ribbon, which meant the person literally had no limits—often a sign of the sub not knowing what their limits were. No dark blue, which stood for heavy or intense sadism and masochism. Maybe it was because he'd dedicated his life to protecting and serving, but Kyler just wasn't into hard-core S&M. Never had been. There was also no brown, which meant she wasn't into pony or animal play. And she wore no orange ribbon, which stood for anal sex. Kyler wondered if that was a hard or soft limit. The only color she wore that gave him any pause was the purple ribbon, which indicated that the club's newest submissive enjoyed breath play.

Kyler's heart kicked into a sprint as his gaze latched onto that purple ribbon. Breath play was some of the riskiest edge play out there—neither safe nor sane in the hands of an inexperienced Dom. Personally, he got off on it because he loved the way it could heighten a submissive's reaction, but he was not only an experienced Dom, but experienced in martial arts training, which taught safe choke and strangle-holds.

Text scrolled on the monitor listing the players out on Blasphemy's floor. A new name popped up: *Mia (unattached submissive)*. Given all of their private rooms and hidden nooks where people could play, keeping an accurate head count was a critical part of their operations.

First names were all most of the Masters got to know about the identity of their members, besides what the players decided to share or reveal about themselves. Privacy and information security were key concerns of their clientele, and Blasphemy guarded their members' identities fiercely. Only Isaac, who'd designed their security systems, and Master Hale, a billionaire businessman who owned a majority interest in the club but rarely played anymore, had access to everyone's complete profiles. The rest of them were on a need-to-know.

On the screen, Mia rose from her chair and shook Griffin's hand.

As if her movement beckoned his, Kyler rose, too, his body making demands his mind hadn't yet settled on. But then his mind fucking caught up.

Mia. Beautiful name, that was for sure, and it certainly fit the woman with all her pretty curves.

Curves his hands itched to caress, hold, grasp.

It'd been months for him, and he was ready. If she wanted to play, he'd play. He adjusted the black leather cuff around his left wrist. The cuff and its hand-stitched silver "M" marked him as one of the club's twelve Masters. Kyler was otherwise one of the more laid-back of the club's Doms, preferring a pair of well-worn black jeans and a partially open black button-down shirt with the sleeves rolled up to his elbows.

"I'm gonna head out," he said.

Isaac smirked over his shoulder. "About damn time. Have fun."

"We'll see," he said, keeping his voice even. Because whether he and this newbie were red hot together or completely ill-suited, he'd still be going home alone.

* * * *

Inside the main part of Blasphemy, Mia immediately felt overwhelmed. Overwhelmed by the beauty, elegance, and decadence of the rehabilitated church, with its massive stained-glass windows, thick marble columns holding up the vaulted ceiling, and soaring frescos on the walls. In the center of the nave sat a large circular bar made out of marble and iron, surrounded by groupings of leather couches and chairs. This was nothing like the club she'd been to before. Everything here screamed money, order, and attention to detail.

Mia was overwhelmed by the very atmosphere of the place, with its low, pulsing, chanting music. Overwhelmed by the moans and cries of ecstasy coming from nearby and further inside, and the idea that she could be the one making those sounds. Soon, if she was lucky. Overwhelmed by the sheer size of the place—not just the central space, all around which pieces of equipment sat with public scenes underway— but also by the rooms and halls that jutted off all along one side of the long space.

Even with all that, the place had a seriously cool vibe that the artist in her already loved.

Despite the fact that a few people had directed interested smiles her way, she wasn't ready to jump right in. She needed a moment to gather her wits about her and get the lay of the land. Ducking her chin, she made for the bar and slipped onto a stool.

"What can I get you?" a deep voice said.

Mia looked up to find a big man with light brown hair and eyes smiling at her. And it was a stunningly sexy smile, one that appeared to be on the cusp of breaking into laughter. It drew her right in. "A glass of champagne, please," she said, the bubbly stuff one of her biggest weaknesses.

He slid a napkin in front of her and nodded. "What's your name?"

"Mia. It's my first time," she added, nerves getting the best of her.

"Yup," he said, putting the flute in front of her. "I never forget a face. It's my superpower." He winked.

Mia laughed. "Is that the only one?"

His expression turned absolutely wicked as he leaned toward her. "Try me sometime and find out." He extended a hand. "I'm Master Quinton, Mia. Nice to meet you. Welcome to Blasphemy."

"Thank you," she said with a grin as they shook. She looked around as she savored her first sips of the bubbly. Sweet and crisp. "This building is absolutely amazing."

Master Quinton braced his hands on the bar top, drawing Mia's gaze to the leather cuff he wore on his left hand. An ornate silver "M" was embroidered into it.

"Shoulda seen it when we first bought it. It had been abandoned for the better part of a decade. Filled with trash and debris. Birds nesting all over the place. But you could still look at it and see it deserved to be saved." He winked at her again, more of that mischievousness in his gaze. "Even if it was for a club like this."

She chuckled, Master Quinton's easy manner and friendliness chasing away the rest of her nerves.

"Excuse me," he said as a waitress in a latex mini-dress with strategically placed cutouts waved for him.

Taking another sip of champagne, Mia's gaze swung around the place—and collided with a tall man leaning against one of the leather couches. Wearing black jeans that showcased strong thighs and a black dress shirt that emphasized the breadth of his shoulders and the size of his biceps, he was so ruggedly sexy that it stole her breath.

Brown hair. Blue eyes. Dominance so palpable in his gaze that Mia found it hard not to look down. Kneel. Submit. From just that one look.

Despite the way his arms were crossed, she could make out the leather cuff on his wrist, like the ones that Master Griffin and Master Quinton wore.

And then he started toward her.

Her heart tripped into a sprint and her body came alive with each step closer he took. He moved with a swagger that communicated confidence and grace, control and agility, like if she fled, he'd easily give chase—and take her down to the ground in an inescapable hold.

She almost wanted to put that theory to the test. But she couldn't. She was frozen to her seat. All she could do was watch him, as if it was all he *wanted* her to do.

By the time he stood in front of her, Mia's skin felt tingly. Her erect nipples pushed against her sheer top, and a dizzying need had settled between her legs.

He slid onto the stool next to her, his knee brushing her thigh. The contact jolted heat through her. Those piercing blue eyes cut to her face. "Mia, I'm Master Kyler. Welcome to Blasphemy." His voice was just deep enough that she could easily imagine it turning into a growl.

She didn't bother to wonder how he knew her name. "Thank you, Master Kyler. I…I've been wanting to come for a while."

"What made you decide to come tonight then?" he asked, turning toward her on his stool.

"Well, uh," she said, almost feeling like she had to shake off the haze of arousal his very presence caused. "Today I finished all the preparations for a big gallery opening I'm hosting on Friday night. I felt like I needed to unwind from the stress of working under my first big deadline in this job."

He nodded, his gaze dropping from her face to her throat to her breasts. His attention snagged there for a second, causing her face to flush, before traveling downward to her thighs, almost indecently bare because of the skirt's short length. And then his eyes flashed back to hers.

And they blazed so hotly with interest that Mia gave in to the urge she'd felt and lowered her gaze.

"Look at me."

She did, instantly and without even a thought. It was pure instinctive reaction. Excitement coiled in her belly because with just that one command, he was already exciting her more than just about anyone she'd ever met in her whole life.

Whatever else he was, Master Kyler was the real thing.

He held out his hand, silently requesting hers. She gave it to him. Because, honestly, with the way he was making her feel, what *wouldn't* she give him? He grasped her wrist and turned her hand palm upward.

His touch was firm without being hurtful, strong, sure. His hand was big, his fingers distractingly calloused. "How long have you been in the lifestyle, Mia?" he asked, the fingers on his free hand perusing the ribbons on her white leather cuff. White, for unattached, unclaimed.

"I realized I was submissive in college, and I had a couple of boyfriends who tried to be dominant when I told them what I was interested in. But it was really in graduate school where I found a community and learned what it meant to be a submissive. That was about five years ago." She gasped as his fingertips dragged over her forearm. She felt the touch *everywhere*, which emphasized exactly how badly she *wanted* it everywhere, making her squirm in her seat.

Master Kyler watched her reaction, fully aware of what he was doing to her. And, good. Because she wasn't sure what might happen between them, but whatever it was, she wanted it. *God*, she needed it.

"May I please ask what the 'M' on your cuff stands for?" Her gaze snagged on the way the worn leather was knotted at the small of his wrist. The fashion was almost medieval, like something a knight might wear under his armor. And it was seriously hot as hell.

"There are twelve Masters at Blasphemy. We founded the club six years ago and we own it jointly. We also set the rules and settle any disputes. In addition to the Dungeon Monitors, you may always come to any of us if you need help or have a concern." He held up his left hand. "Do you like my cuff?"

She nodded, even as heat flooded into her face. Because, busted. Though, of all the things he might've caught her ogling about him, she supposed his cuff was among the lesser embarrassing to admit to. "Yes."

"Yes...?" He nailed her with a stare.

"Yes, Sir," she rushed out.

"And why do you like it?" he asked, shifting toward her. Most of his body invaded the space of hers. But not nearly enough.

"Because it's hot," she said. "Sir."

One side of his mouth slipped into a grin, and if she'd thought his serious face was hot—and it really freaking was—his face with a little humor shaping it was jarringly gorgeous. She'd probably be stunned to see a full-out smile. "Is it, now?"

She smirked at him, her belly doing a little flip as she contemplated sassing him. "Are you fishing for compliments, Master Kyler?"

And then it happened. That full-out smile, and deep laughter to boot. A nearly killer combination. One that revealed that there was a good sense of humor underneath all that intensity.

He shrugged with one shoulder. "Maybe I am. What man wouldn't want to be complimented by a beautiful woman like you?"

Just like that, the intensity returned. In mind-boggling spades. Even though the hint of a smile still played around his mouth. And, *oh*, his mouth. Full lips. A small scar above the right side of his top one. A harshness to the set of his jaw that communicated dominance and authority without him having to say a word.

"Thank you, Sir," she managed.

"Would you like to find a spot to talk more privately, Mia?" he asked.

Butterflies swooped through her. Because yes. Yes to the millionth power. "I would, Sir."

He got off the stool, his grip on her wrist changing until he was holding her hand, his big palm completely engulfing hers. Champagne glass in hand, she followed. And then he was guiding them through the rectangular space, revealing more and more of Blasphemy's secrets to her. A fuck bench with a grouping of couches around it for watching. A bondage chair with a male submissive tied up, the rope in a series of crisscrosses over his chest. A woman restrained in upright stocks, her Domme spanking her with a nasty-looking paddle. An ornately carved St. Andrew's cross, the wood somehow looking like it fit naturally among all the old marble.

Master Kyler led her to the side of the room, into the dimmer space under the second-floor balcony, illuminated here and there with torches on tall iron sconces. When they turned the corner into the shielded hallway, Mia suddenly found her back pressed into the cool marble. The Dom pinned her wrist against her chest, his fingertips just brushing the bottom of her throat. Arousal lanced through her so hard and so fast that the thong she wore left no doubt that she was wet.

"I can't decide if I love or hate that fucking skirt," Master Kyler said, his blue eyes piercing, suddenly stormy.

Yes! Yes! Yes! Heart pounding, Mia smiled, even as she dropped her gaze. "Does it not please you, Master Kyler?"

He hummed and leaned in even closer. "Look at me." His gaze ran over her face, like he was studying her, reading her, seeing all of her. And, *God*, his scent—soap and leather and something quintessentially male—was more intoxicating than the champagne. "It might please me too well."

For a moment, something that looked like a frown flashed across his expression, and then it was gone again. He pulled her from the wall and took her hand once more. At the end of the secluded hall, a couch and table sat alone, the little nook deliciously private.

He settled into the corner of the couch, and his grip on her hand tightened as she moved to sit beside him. Stilling, she met his gaze.

"I would like you to sit on my lap. I'd like to hold you while we talk. But I'd understand if you'd prefer a little distance for now, so you are free to say no."

Mia's gaze swept over his body—his broad shoulders, his lean abdomen, his hard thighs. Her body knew where it wanted to be, even if her mind needed a moment to work up the courage to admit it. "I'd like that, Sir."

His expression filled with satisfaction, and then he scooped her off her heels and put her in his lap.

The move was so unexpected that she couldn't help but laugh, throwing her head back like a kid riding a roller coaster, just along for the thrilling ride of it.

"Liked that, did you?" he asked, giving her that sexy smile again.

Grinning, she nodded, but for a moment, she couldn't talk. Because her senses were absolutely swimming in him. His hardness against all her softness. The press of what felt like a deliciously long cock against her ass. The possessive curl of his arm around the small of her back. His face so close to hers.

"Good," he said, his expression shifting into all that serious intensity again. "So did I. And you feel fucking phenomenal against me. But now I need to know, Mia—would you just like to chat, or would you like to talk about playing? Tonight. With me."

Chapter 3

Kyler wanted to play with this new little submissive. Badly. He enjoyed her laugh, the honesty in her eyes, the hourglass shape of her beautiful body. Satisfaction flooded through him at the solid weight of her in his lap, at the flared curve of her hips, absolutely perfect for grabbing, holding, restraining.

Mia licked her lips, the action drawing his gaze and leaving the red-painted skin wet, shiny. "I…I'd like to talk about playing." She said the words quietly, as if they weren't easy for her to admit, but he still respected the hell out of her being able to be direct about what she wanted.

He gave a tight nod. "I'm glad to hear that. What would you like to know about me?" he asked, curious to see what she'd think important to know about a new Dom.

She tilted her head, her gaze running over his face before quickly dropping. "You said you helped co-found this club six years ago. How long have you been a Dom? Did you have specific training?"

Kyler was glad to see her starting with such basic questions because it meant she was thinking about her own safety and well-being. "I got into the lifestyle in my mid-twenties, so, about a decade ago, but I'd realized this was something I needed even before that. It was like the difference between a kiss that was nice and one that set your blood on fire, between hugging a friend and being pressed up against someone who you'd sell your soul to get inside of. Once I started realizing those needs, seeing them for what they were, I sought out the community. A Dom with years of experience gave me a lot of guidance, and I joined a club that offered workshops and mentorship for newbie Doms. And I bottomed for a Domme at that club because I wanted to experience what that was like firsthand."

"It's always interesting to hear how other people come to this," Mia said, her fingers toying with the back of his hair. Kyler leaned into the touch. Suddenly, she pulled her hand away. "I'm sorry, Sir."

He caught her wrist and brought her hand to his mouth. Kissed the tender, sensitive cup of her palm. "Don't be. You can touch me. We're not in scene right now, Mia. It felt good." More than good, if he was being honest. And in a comforting, almost familiar way at that. Something he didn't much experience.

She gave a little nod and settled her arm around his shoulder again, her hand falling against the back of his neck, her fingertips playing with his hair.

"What else?" he asked, stroking his fingers over the sheer white lace covering her shoulder. He usually preferred more skin showing, but this top looked fucking amazing on her—highlighting the perfect curves and cleavage of her large breasts and the warm tone of her skin.

"Do you have any special rules or expectations of a submissive?"

His fingers traced the line of the deep V-neck on her shirt. Satisfaction roared through him as her mouth parted and her eyelids momentarily closed. "I have one primary rule—honesty. A D/s relationship is based on trust—your trust that I will take care of you and your needs and respect your limits, and my trust that your reactions while playing are genuine and that you'll be truthful when something is too much for you physically or emotionally. That doesn't mean I wouldn't push your boundaries if I thought you could handle it or if we'd talked about doing so, but it does mean that I would *always* listen to your safe words, which means I'd need to know that you'd use them. What are they?" he asked, knowing this was part of what Master Griffin would've discussed with her.

"Yellow for slow down or wait, and red for stop," she said immediately.

"Good. Do you have a problem speaking up for yourself during a scene and using your safe words, Mia?" Kyler kept his gaze locked on her eyes. Nothing but honesty there.

"No," she said.

"Have you ever used a safe word during a scene?"

"Yes. It's how I know I'm not a masochist. I was curious what a more intense S&M scene would be like. As soon as it started to heat up, it scared the hell out of me. It hurt, and not in a pain-that-becomes-pleasurable kinda way."

Kyler was glad that wasn't her kink, because he wouldn't be able to give it to her. And the idea of sending her in the direction of Master Zeke didn't make him happy at all. Not one bit. Where the possessive urge came from, Kyler didn't know. It sure as shit wasn't like him. "Did the Dom stop?"

She frowned, and anger curled into Kyler's gut. Because he knew what the answer was before she said it. "Not right away."

"Fuck, I'm sorry."

"Thank you. I'm okay about it. Now," she added.

On instinct, Kyler pressed a kiss to her forehead. "You can trust me to take care of you, Mia." Sitting back, his gaze swept down her face, enjoying the pleased expression she wore. From the promise of his words or the kiss? He laid his hand against her sternum and slowly slid his palm upward until his thumb and fingers separated around the base of her throat. He applied just the slightest amount of pressure there.

She sucked in a breath, and that one reaction surged blood into his cock. Mia squirmed, rocketing his arousal even further.

"Be still," he gritted out.

She froze, her eyes on his.

"How important is the breath play to you?"

Her eyes dilated, her expression read as needy, and her breathing quickened. Her obvious excitement went a long way toward answering the question. And these reactions were exactly what he loved about it. But did she *need* it?

"I don't have to have it, but..." She looked down, her lashes fanning out against her skin.

"Look at me and finish that sentence," he said, his voice full of grit. Because against his fingers, her pulse was flying.

"But it probably excites me more than anything else, and it gets me off faster than anything else," she said, her cheeks turning beautifully pink.

"Does it now?" Not that he really needed to ask. His grip tightened, just a little.

"Yes, Sir," she whispered, her voice breathy, full of desire.

"Say my name," he said, wanting to hear it with all that arousal coloring her tone.

"Yes, Master Kyler."

Fucking hell.

In a quick move, he slid his hand up her back and fisted her ponytail, tugging her head backward and her whole body closer. Hand still gripping her throat, he shifted them so that she was almost reclining, allowing him to look down into her face.

And he thought her pulse had been flying before.

"You like to be choked?"

"Yes, Sir."

"Choked to the point of not being able to breathe?"

"Yes, Sir."

His grip tightened. "Gagged?"

"Yes. Sir," she added, as if she'd momentarily forgotten protocol.

Jesus Christ, his cock was like fucking steel. "Asphyxiated to the point of passing out?" he asked, his gut twisting.

"I've never done that. The idea of it..."

He nailed her with a stare, allowing her the time to gather the words the little furrow in her brow said she was looking for.

"It both excites me and scares me, but I'm not sure which more."

"Thank you for the honesty. I won't go that far, Mia. I won't put plastic over your head and I won't duct tape your mouth. I also won't use any bondage position that hangs you primarily by the throat or neck. If any of those are things you need, I won't be able to give them to you," he said, hoping like hell she didn't need them. Occasionally, he had a moment of discomfort—maybe even cognitive dissonance—about the fact that he was both a cop *and* a Dom who got off on bondage and submission and spanking and even role-playing scenarios that flirted with non-consent. Because he'd seen the trauma real abuse caused. But what he did was safe, sane, and consensual, and he drew the line where any of those three might be compromised, which in his opinion included the edgier breath play.

A fast shake of her head. "No. I don't want any of that. I just want—" Her eyes went wide.

"What, little one?" Satisfaction at her answer mixed with curiosity about what she'd not said. He needed to know.

Her throat worked under his hand in a hard swallow. "You."

The word hit him like a blowtorch, licking molten heat over his skin and his cock. "Then tell me now. Do you have any further questions?"

"Are...are you in any kind of relationship with another submissive?" she managed.

The questions she'd asked had been smart, informed, and got at the core of a D/s relationship, even a temporary one built around only a single scene. What she'd asked said a lot about who she was—and what he knew of her so far, he liked. A fucking lot. "No. And I'm not looking for one either." He arched a brow.

She gave a nod, her expression unchanging. Perfect.

"Anything else?" he asked, keeping that brow arched. Damnit all to hell, but the arousal in her eyes and the heat roaring off her body were stunning. "Anything you don't want to have happen that I should know about?"

"No," she whispered.

He squeezed her throat.

"No, Sir," she rushed out.

His body vibrated with need for this little submissive. "Then rise, strip, and let me inspect you. Now."

* * * *

Mia was nearly dizzy with lust, and Master Kyler had barely touched her. But, Jesus, he gave some seriously good mental foreplay. Because his words and the look in his eyes had done as much as his hand on her throat to make her body and her pussy absolutely ache with need.

And damn my luck that he's not looking for a relationship.

But in this moment, that didn't matter. All that mattered was Master Kyler. And pleasing him. And learning all the ways he might please her.

Moving as quickly and as gracefully as she could, Mia sat up and unzipped her ankle boots. Sat them aside. And then she rose to stand in front of Sir, wanting her stripping to be pleasurable for him, too. Turning to him reminded her that they were at the end of a long hallway where anyone might walk by. Watching and being watched felt dirty and naughty and a little scary to her, and it had always ramped up her arousal. Heart racing, pulse thumping, Mia lifted the white lace over her head and placed it on the table. She smoothed her hands over her full breasts before reaching behind her to unclasp the sheer bra. And then she gave him her back as she let the skirt slide down her legs, baring her ass to him, before letting her black satin thong join the latex on the floor. Spreading her legs, she bent at the waist to retrieve the clothing.

"Freeze. Hold that position," Master Kyler said from behind her.

"You have a fucking gorgeous ass, Mia."

"Thank you, Sir." Her speech was shaky as she grasped her ankles, the clothing all in one hand. The grit in his voice revealed the truth in his words, and satisfaction that she pleased him spread warmth through her even as her nerves made it hard to stand still. It had been months since her last lover, and no one had ever affected her as deeply as Master Kyler, who'd made her wet before he'd hardly touched her.

Big hands smoothed up her thighs and grasped her ass. And then he spanked her. One cheek then the other. She gasped at the impacts, the sting immediately heating her skin—and her core. He rubbed where he'd smacked, and then he spanked her again, his big hand landing in different places and sending jolts of pain and pleasure through her. More rubbing, and then he grasped her cheeks again, his thumbs sweeping between, just brushing over her anus, before squeezing and pulling her cheeks apart. He lifted and squeezed, the motion tugging at her pussy, too. A shiver raced over her skin at the rush of sensations.

"So wet already," he said, his voice low and full of approval. Just the sound of it made her wetter. He palmed her lower back, his thumb falling between her cheeks, the pad of it laying against her rear entrance. The touch made her gasp, but he didn't push further. "Has anyone ever had your ass, Mia?"

"No, Sir." Because she'd never gotten close enough with anyone to want to give them that part of herself, too. But now, knowing he was examining the most intimate parts of her, she found herself debating, wishing, wanting. No doubt Master Kyler would make her hot enough to make it good.

"Is it a hard limit for you?" he asked, his other hand reaching between her legs to caress the front of her body—her nipples, the valley between her breasts, her belly.

"Maybe not with the right person, Sir," she managed, desire flooding through her. Just talking to this man was insanely erotic. How did he do that? As his hand explored her, his corded forearm rubbed against her mound, just teasing her clit and lips, making her desperate for actual friction.

Master Kyler hummed, and then his forearm was dragging firmly against her clit as his arm retreated until his fingers were right there and stroking her in maddening circles, once, twice, three times.

Mia let out a deep moan and her legs shook.

The touch disappeared, and she moaned again, desperately now, ready to beg for more, for anything, for everything.

Behind her, Master Kyle chuckled. The sexy bastard. "Rise for my inspection."

She rose and turned around to find him standing, arms crossed, biceps thick under the taut material of his shirt, his expression stern as he examined her. Legs spread, she laced her hands behind her head and waited for his next command. It had been a while since she'd last stood before a Dom like this and accepted his unflinching observation. She'd almost forgotten the rush of it, the overwhelming mix of anticipation and nerves and arousal. Without her heels on, he had a good five inches on her. She tried to keep her eyes forward, even though what she wanted to do was drink him in the way he was doing to her. As a man, he was seriously hot. That he was also a Dom almost blew her mind.

"Mmm, fucking beautiful," Master Kyler said, his gaze raking over her. Slowly, he walked around her, one full circle, before stopping in front of her again. "Tits out, Mia." She corrected her posture, thrusting her chest out. "There it is. Very good." Pleasure flooded through her.

He stepped so close that if she took a deep breath, her breasts would probably push into him. And, God, she wanted that contact so damn bad.

Looming over her, his gaze bore into hers. He leaned down, bringing their mouths close together. Close enough that she felt his exhale. She wanted to beg him to kiss her. The words were right on the tip of her tongue. But she feared if she did, he would punish her for speaking out of turn. So she waited. The seconds dragged on and on until Mia was panting from his proximity alone, from the anticipation of what he'd do, from fighting her own urges and needs.

"What a good girl you are," he whispered. She hadn't even fully vocalized the moan that spilled out of her before his mouth was on hers. Hard. Claiming. Deliciously overwhelming. His hand grabbed her by the throat as his tongue penetrated her mouth, tasting her and moving in and out of her.

She wanted to embrace him, cling to him, climb him, but she held the inspection position even though she was shaking with the effort of her restraint.

"Fuck," he gritted out as he pulled back. Gaze still glued hard to hers, one hand still gripping her throat, he reached between her legs and rubbed there. "Your bareness here pleases me."

"Thank you, Sir," she said, so glad she'd taken the time to shave...everything.

His hand disappeared for a moment, and then there was a buzzing noise. That was all she'd registered before strong vibrations clamped down on her clit. She cried out.

"I want to see what your face looks like when you come, little Mia," Master Kyler said, his hand tightening around her neck. He shifted his grip, and his fingers applied a hard pressure against the side of her throat. She gasped for air, and her effort to breathe made a light rasping noise that felt like it was hardwired to her clit. Arousal closed in on her in a tight spiral of need. The combination of the vibrator and the choking and that strange pressure and the raw masculinity shaping his handsome face immediately shoved Mia toward the edge.

"When you're ready, you don't have to ask. Just come," he said, the vibrator on her clit pressing more firmly, circling. She couldn't help but tilt her hips to get more friction. Her breathing rasped louder.

"Keep your eyes open," he said, and then he kissed her. It was strange, kissing someone while looking into their eyes. Strange, but also hugely intimate.

But it didn't take her long to realize that his kiss had an ulterior motive. Because now, between his chokehold and the kiss, she was getting very little air. Her lungs burned. A kernel of panic lit in her belly. A strange light-headedness settled over the edges of her brain.

It was utter fucking perfection.

A guttural moan ripped out of her despite the fact that Master Kyler was still kissing her. He pulled back, allowing more air to surge into her lungs as her body detonated in the most amazing orgasm she'd had...maybe ever. It went on and on, Master Kyler not letting up on her throat or her clit.

A shudder ripped through her body and her knees suddenly went soft. In a flash, his hand released her throat and his arm wrapped around her lower back. "I've got you," he said.

"Thank you, Sir," she said, leaning into him, absolutely stunned by how amazing that'd been. "Thank you."

He tugged her tighter against him and guided her head to his shoulder. His height allowed him to tuck her in just beneath his chin, which felt so nice.

"That's it. Lean on me. Just take a moment." His hand stroked over her shoulder, her arm, the side of her breast. After a few minutes, he asked, "Steadier?"

"Yes, Sir."

"Good. Unbutton my shirt, Mia."

"Ooh, okay," she said, unthinkingly. "I mean—"

He chuckled. "We'll consider that slip caused by post-orgasmic haze."

She grinned up at him, her fingers making quick work of the buttons. "Absolutely, Master Kyler."

"Now take the shirt off."

Mia slid the dress shirt down his arms, and it was a whole freaking lot like opening a Christmas present. Because Master Kyler had tattoos all down his shoulders and upper arms. He also had a series of nasty-looking scars all over his right shoulder, red enough that they appeared at least somewhat recent. Instead of detracting from his appeal, they made him seem rougher, maybe even dirtier. His muscles were sculpted without being overbuilt, defined without bulging. Brown hair lightly covered the hard pads of his pecs and the ridges of his abdomen. She wanted to lick him. Everywhere.

He let her look her fill, satisfaction making his expression smug, almost arrogant, and then he finally said, "Undo my pants and take out my cock."

A crazy, tingly feeling whipped through Mia's chest. "Yes, Sir," she whispered, opening his fly and taking his long, hard length in hand. *God*, he was a delicious handful. She gripped him. Stroked.

He caught her wrist. "Greedy girl. On your knees. Hands behind your back."

Licking her lips as she got into position, Mia was already dying to feel him in her mouth. Had she ever wanted a man this bad? Had she ever been this ravenous for a taste? Had there ever been anyone like Master Kyler in her life before?

Shoving his jeans down to mid-thigh, Master Kyler peered down at her, his expression fierce and raw and even a little harsh. "Suck my cock, Mia."

On a moan, she leaned forward and swallowed his long cock. When she'd taken most of him, his hand landed in her hair, fisting her ponytail and controlling her movements. His dick was heavy and demanding against her tongue, against the back of her throat, and she loved his taste, the way the size of him was almost too much, the way it wasn't nearly enough.

"Eyes on me." His expression was hunger personified. The thrill of it made her moan. He set a pace fucking her face, going deep, but nothing she couldn't handle. She sucked as hard as she could, loving the dominance in the way he handled her, in the way he *took* his pleasure from her. "More," he said, voice rough. His free hand grasped her jaw.

Mia tilted her head back, further opening her throat, and stuck her tongue out around his cock, taking more. His head closed off her throat on each deep thrust, and the aggressiveness of it awakened need between her legs again. Truly amazing given how shattering her orgasm had been.

His grip in her hair and under her jaw tightened. "More, Mia. If you can't take all of me here, you can't have me anywhere else."

A strangled moan ripped out of her as she impaled the back of her throat on his cock, using her legs to press her upper body forward so that she could force more of him into her mouth. Satisfaction rolled through her when her lips clamped around the base of his cock and her nose pressed hard against his lower stomach.

"Yes, yes, fucking yes." The raw satisfaction in his voice flooded her with pride, even as he held his cock there, cutting off her breath, threatening to gag her, igniting that kernel of panic again. Her hands fisted and unfisted behind her back until she was fighting the urge to push against his thighs. "Good girl," he said, withdrawing quickly from her mouth, his words almost a growl.

Mia gulped air, the breath sawing into her, saliva wetting her lips.

Master Kyler leaned down and thumbed away the wetness beneath her eyes she hadn't even realized was there. "You okay?"

"Yes, Sir," she said, her chest warming at him checking in with her. This guy was clearly one of the good ones.

One of the good ones who doesn't want a relationship...

He grasped her chin and tilted her head up to meet his gaze. For a long moment, he just looked at her, his expression like he was waging some internal debate. His lips pressed into a thin line until he finally spoke. "Tell me, Mia, where do you want me to come? In your mouth or in your pussy?"

The answer was instinctive. "Whatever would most please you,

Master Kyler." Though, in case his "no relationship" stance meant this would be their only time together, she would sincerely hate not to have had him inside her. Just once.

"I asked you a direct question for your preference. Answer me."

Excitement whipped through her belly and coiled the need between her legs even tighter. "My pussy, Sir."

Somehow, she was on her feet in an instant. He'd lifted her by her arms like she weighed nothing, despite the fact that she wasn't a petite woman.

"Then stand facing the wall and spread your feet."

"Yes, Sir," Mia said, already moving. And then all she could do was wait.

Chapter 4

Be careful, Kyler thought as he retrieved a condom from the bowl on the table. He rolled it on, his gaze glued to how fucking perfect Mia looked against the wall. Waiting for him.

The warning wasn't about his treatment of the submissive, it was about how much she was intriguing him. When he'd asked for her preference regarding the scene, he'd been torn about how he wanted her to answer. Because he wasn't sure whether fucking would satisfy the urge he felt to be with her once and for all—or just make him yearn for more.

The fact that there was even a question for him was sending up some red flags.

Don't overthink it, Vance. It's just because you've been out of the scene for more than three months.

Maybe. It was definitely longer than he'd gone without playing in a long, long time. That much was true.

Approaching her, Kyler shoved his jeans further down his legs. He wanted her to feel the rough sensation of the denim against her thighs. He stood behind her, purposely looming, wanting to raise her anticipation of what was going to happen and when, how he'd first touch her. Leaning in, he blew against the side of her neck. Mia startled, making him smile. Yeah, she was wound about as tight as he was. Satisfaction rolled through him.

"Hands on the wall and arch your back," he said.

She complied immediately, her hands by her head, her round bottom jutting toward him.

He spanked one cheek, then the other, loving the bloom of pink. "Arch more. Stick that beautiful fucking ass out." She did, and he rewarded her with two more spanks. "Yes."

And then he backed off. Looked his fill. He didn't want to rush this. And he wanted her desperate for him.

He retrieved the little finger vibrator he'd used before and turned it on. The muscles of her back tightened at the sound, just enough to reveal she was on edge. He reached between her legs and pressed it tight against her clit.

A moan ripped out of her. He held it there for a long moment and dragged his fingers lightly down her back. She shuddered.

"Be still," he said in a low voice.

Rubbing the vibrator in small circles, Kyler brushed feather-light fingertips over her shoulders, down her arm, down her ribs. She flinched, clearly ticklish.

"I said to be still," he said, removing the vibrator. She made a significantly less pleased sound, and he grinned, glad she couldn't see his amusement.

"Mmm, Mia. I have to say, you look so good standing there that I could just jerk off at the sight. Shoot my come all over that ass." He returned the vibrator to the arm of the couch.

"No, *please*," she said.

Kyler was on her in an instant, his body pressing her hard up against the marble, his cock grinding against her rear, his hands pinning hers to the wall. "What did you say?" he asked, his lips at her ear.

A quick shake of her head.

"I know I heard you say something, Mia," he said. God*damn*, her soft, luscious curves felt fantastic against all his hardness.

"I...I just..."

"Did you beg me?" he asked.

"Yes, Sir," she whispered.

"Mmm, yes you did. Do it again. Beg me, Mia."

"Please...please come *in* me, Master Kyler."

He rocked his hips, slowly fucking her lush cheeks. "More." He bit the shell of her ear.

Mia gasped. "Please fuck me, Master. Please. I need you so bad."

The raw desire in her voice wrapped itself around his body so hard that he didn't correct her. "Master" used alone without his name attached to it implied a commitment between them they didn't have. He wasn't *her* Master. At least not beyond this scene. And he couldn't be.

"Please, Sir," she said again. Voices sounded from down the hallway, and Kyler really only noticed because Mia's head cocked to the right just enough to register that she'd heard, too.

"Do you mind people watching you, Mia?" he asked, stroking his erection, his fist knocking against her ass.

"No, Sir," she said, her voice strained with arousal. Goosebumps erupted on her neck and shoulders. Interesting.

"Do you *like* people watching you?" he asked, guessing at the answer from the way her hands clenched against the wall.

She released a shaky breath. "Yes, Sir, I do."

Damn. *Damn.* He'd always been very visual, and watching and being watched had always gotten him hot. And she liked it, too. This woman was flipping all his switches. One by fucking one. "What a dirty girl you are. You want people to see my cock sliding into your pussy? You want them to hear you screaming and coming?" He stepped closer and guided his cock between her legs.

"God, yes. Sir."

Damn, he loved the honesty in her voice, her reactions, her body. "Then let the whole fucking club watch, because I can't wait to bury myself in you." He penetrated her wet heat, inch by scalding inch, until he was balls deep. Jesus Christ.

"Yes, yes, yes, yes," she babbled, pushing back on him.

He gripped her hands hard. "Be still, goddamnit." Because he was strung really fucking tight right now, and it had been months, and she was pushing him. Hard.

Sonofabitch. This one was trouble.

Of the best and worst kind.

Tilting his hips, he slowly withdrew, and then he hammered home. Slowly withdrew, then hammered home. Her anticipation of the deep thrusts vibrated around them like a physical thing, and her screams of pleasure were going to live in his dreams.

"Feel how you take me," Kyler gritted out, his mouth still against her ear, his hands and body still pinning her to the wall. Withdraw and thrust. Withdraw and thrust. "Take me, Mia."

"Yes, Sir. Yes, yes."

Words demanded to be voiced, words Kyler really shouldn't say. But they came out anyway. "Whose pussy is this, Mia?" Hard thrust.

"Yours, Sir," she said. No hesitation. It fucking slayed him.

"Louder. Let them hear you."

"*Yours, Sir,*" she shouted.

Satisfaction roared through him like a drug he'd mainlined. He wrapped his arm around her throat in a classic chokehold. "And whose throat is this?"

"Yours, Sir. Oh, God," she cried out.

"That's. Fucking. Right." Without any warning, he wrapped his other arm around her belly and lifted her, her pussy still impaled on his cock. Carrying her against him, he took about ten steps backward to plant his ass on the couch again. He sat at the edge so he could lean back with her on top of him, and so he could use his thighs to hammer his cock into that sweet cunt.

Arm still tight around her neck, Kyler placed open-mouthed kisses against her ear, her cheek, her temple. He absolutely loved her weight on top of him, her thighs falling open on the outside of his.

"I want your hands on me. Anywhere you want," he growled. "Now."

Moaning, Mia's fingernails on one hand dug into his forearm where it gripped her throat. Her other arm fell back to wrap around his head, her hand in his hair, gripping and pulling. Fuck.

He choked her tighter, and her pussy clamped down on his cock. He wanted her to come again, to come all over him, to absolutely soak his cock and balls with the pleasure he gave her.

He grasped the vibrator and reached around to her clit. She screamed when the vibrations hit her, the orgasm making her back bow against him, her tits pushing out and demanding attention. With his free hand, he grasped a nipple, squeezed, twisted. And the orgasm just kept going.

Finally, she slumped on top of him.

"We're. Not. Done." He pushed her off of him. "On your stomach." He barely let her lay down on the couch before he was on her, his weight covering her, his cock right back inside her, his hand clamped around her throat and forcing her head back.

"Oh, Master Kyler," she rasped, the sound tortured because of the way he was holding her. "Harder, please."

"Harder where?" he asked, moving inside her.

"Everywhere, Sir," she said. "Please."

"Yeah, I know what you need." Handling her throat as hard as he was willing, he cut off her breathing almost all the way, his hips snapping against her ass as he nailed her. And she took it. She took all of him. His weight. His hold. His cock.

He felt the vibrations of her strangled scream before he heard it. And then she was coming. Coming hard. And so was he. The orgasm rushed down his spine and exploded outward again, just absolutely shattering him in the best possible way. He moved through it until he couldn't, until he just had to give in to the bone-bending pleasure. He had only enough awareness to remove his hand from her throat, and then his muscles relaxed until she was bearing all of him. Every last piece of him.

"Jesus fucking Christ," he finally gritted out, his chest heaving. "Stay right there, baby." With effort, he eased off of her and stood. He disposed of the condom and the used vibrator in their respective receptacles behind the couch, then pulled up his jeans, leaving them undone. And then he retrieved a blanket from the shelf under the table. Returning to Mia, he crouched beside her. "Sit up for me?"

Her eyes were glassy, expression slack. She complied, but her movements were sluggish, imprecise.

Kyler pulled the blanket around her shoulders, checking her throat for marks as he did. Some redness, but no bruising. He sat next to her, then shifted her into his lap. She was limp on top of him, and he took a moment to tuck the blanket closed over her skin wherever he could. "Talk to me, Mia."

She swallowed once, twice. "I…um…"

He stroked her face. "Are you okay?"

A shudder wracked through her. "Yes, Sir," she whispered.

"Look at me, please," he said, cupping her cheek in his hand. And he thought *he'd* been shattered. Damn, she'd dropped hard, hadn't she? Submissives often achieved a psychological state during an intense scene, particularly one involving pain, that made them feel floaty or euphoric or detached. But afterward, they could crash down from that high. Hard. Kyler imagined the choking did that for her, in spades. "I'm going to get you some food and drink, Mia."

She nodded.

Kyler pushed a button built into the corner of the table. Within a minute, a tall, thin male submissive named Jon, serving as a waiter, appeared next to the couch. "How may I be of service, Sir?"

"Please bring us two bottles of water, a glass of orange juice, and a plate of the cookies," he said, stroking Mia's hair.

"Right away, Sir." The man disappeared.

"Just rest for a minute," Kyler said, cradling her against him. "I've got you." The fact that she'd achieved such a high with him made him feel ten feet tall—and made him pretty fucking protective toward her, too.

The waiter returned within a few minutes. "Here you are, Sir," he said, placing their order on the table.

"Thank you, Jon." The man departed with a nod. Kyler grabbed the waters and handed her one. "Drink this, Mia."

Sluggishly, she tilted the bottle to her lips. Swallowed. Then drank more greedily.

When he was satisfied that she was perking up, he took a long pull from his own bottle. "Better?" he asked.

"Yes, Sir." She wiped at her lips with the back of her hand. "Thank you."

"You're welcome," Kyler said, reaching for the juice and cookies. "Have some of this, too." He placed the plate on her lap and handed her the glass.

"Oh, my God. Are these chocolate chip?" Her smile warmed and reassured him.

Kyler chuckled. "Is there *any other* kind of cookie? I mean, really."

Mia laughed and shook her head. "I agree completely, Sir."

"Good. That's always the best course of action."

She barked out a throaty laugh around a bite. "Oh, is that so?"

The sparkle was back in her dark eyes again, easing the tension in his shoulders. He waggled his eyebrows as he enjoyed his own bite. "Mmhmm."

"I'll keep that in mind."

"You better," he said, winking. Though his brain was already questioning whether she'd need to keep anything in mind where he was concerned. Because those red flags? They were waving at him like fucking crazy.

He liked Mia, as a submissive and as a person. And he barely knew her.

Don't get attached.

Right.

And there was one way to ensure that.

So even as Kyler gave her the aftercare she needed—and that he needed to give her—he already knew the truth. This was the only time he was playing with Mia. It couldn't happen again.

* * * *

At work on Friday, Kyler was feeling antsy, restless, bored out of his fucking mind. The pile of paperwork covering his desk beckoned his attention, but it was the absolute last thing he wanted to be doing.

He wanted to be out on the streets, investigating a case, dominating Mia.

Wait.

What. The. Fuck.

Get your fucking head screwed on right, Vance.

Problem was, his head was screwed all right. Not even forty-eight hours had passed since he'd seen Mia into a cab outside Club Diablo, the public part of their business, and Kyler couldn't stop thinking about her. About how fulfilling playing with her had been. About how many times she'd made him laugh as they'd sat talking for the better part of an hour after their scene ended. About how hard it was to see her go— especially knowing he wouldn't be seeing her again. At least, not as her Dom.

And that was the other part of the reason he couldn't get her out of his head. Assuming he *did* see her again at Blasphemy, she was going to be playing with someone else. And that…that really fucking sucked. And pissed him off. And had made him a miserable sonofabitch to be around.

As if being assigned to a desk buried in paperwork wasn't making him miserable enough. And his shooting practice hadn't gone as well as he wanted earlier today, either.

Damn it all to hell.

He needed a distraction of the non-Blasphemy kind. Because if Mia was there tonight, the last thing he needed was to see her—or see her with anyone else.

Kyler debated, and then an idea came to mind. "Luck be on my side," he said as he found Jeremy Rixey's number in his contacts and dialed. The guy was a fantastic tattoo artist and owned the Hard Ink Tattoo shop across town. It had been closed for most of the summer following an attack that left a big part of the building damaged, but they'd reopened full time just last week.

"Jeremy Rixey here," he answered.

"Jer, it's Kyler Vance. How are you?"

"Yo, Detective. I have all my hair again so everything's good."

Kyler laughed and respected the hell out of the guy for being able to joke about it. In the same shooting incident that had injured Kyler, Jeremy had been pistol-whipped, and the brain injury he'd suffered had necessitated surgery, so his head had been shaved. Kyler had seen Jer at his older brother's wedding a few weeks before, but his dark brown hair had still been pretty short. The guy had been through a lot. "Hair is good."

"Hair is damn good. I think half my personality was in my hair," he said, voice full of humor. "But I'm sure you didn't call to talk about my stunning good looks."

"Well, if there's any chance you have an opening tonight, I'll talk about your good looks as much as you like," Kyler said, forcing nonchalance into his tone when he really wanted this to happen.

"Oh, yeah? Uh, I should be done with my last client around 8:30. If that's not too late, I could work on you then," Jeremy said.

"Don't you close at nine?"

"Yeah, but after everything, you're family. You in?"

Kyler nodded, really appreciating the sentiment. The Rixeys were good people. "I'll be there."

"Great. I'll let everyone know you're coming," Jer said. Everyone meaning his brother, Nick, and the whole group of people Kyler had teamed up with to take down some of the worst scum operating in Baltimore—hell, in the world, given the worldwide scope of their criminal operations.

"Sounds good," Kyler said. He'd no more than hung up, for the first time all day feeling a little bit of contentment, when potentially bad news arrived at his desk.

"Vance," Captain Burkett said, dropping into the chair beside him. "Commissioner Breslin would like to see you at five."

"What for?" Kyler asked. "And why do you look like you've just been to war and back?" The guy was looking rough—tired eyes, haggard expression, sloped shoulders. This investigation wasn't just tough on Kyler, was it.

His captain gulped at a Styrofoam cup of coffee. "Because that's what this place is sometimes. And you know exactly what the commissioner wants to talk about." The man arched a brow.

"Fine," Kyler said, giving a tight nod. It would be his first time meeting Breslin one-on-one. The guy might be a hardass, but Kyler respected that the man was trying to bring some order back to a department that had been spinning out of control, so he had to be a good guy on some level. "You should take some time off, Cap. You kinda look like hell. And this is coming from a guy who knows what hell looks like, so…"

Burkett shook his head. "I'll take time off when I retire."

Kyler chuffed out a doubtful breath. "And when will that be?"

"When I die." Burkett winked and left.

Time crawled until a little before five, and then Kyler found himself in a posh waiting room outside the commissioner's office. Kyler had even put on a jacket and tie over his dress shirt. Good first impressions and all that.

"Detective Vance? Commissioner Breslin will see you now," Natasha, his receptionist, said. She gestured toward the carved wooden door.

Heaving a deep breath, Kyler got up and went inside.

"Have a seat, Detective," Breslin said from behind his own desk. Standing at the window, the older man was looking out at the grit and gleam of Baltimore.

"Yes, sir." Kyler took a seat, and then the commissioner turned and took his own place at his desk.

The man had graying brown hair, a distinguished face, and dark eyes. His voice was gruff and his bearing was authoritative without being arrogant. "I've asked you here today because I'm trying to meet everyone in the department individually. Best way to get to know the place and, more importantly, the people. How long have you been with BPD, Detective?"

Kyler definitely respected the leadership style this represented. An organization—*any* organization—was only as strong as its people. "Little over ten years, sir."

Breslin flipped open a folder in front of him. "That's a long commitment."

"I love what I do. Worked my way up from rookie cop." Kyler laced his hands over his gut.

"And you come from a police family, too," Breslin observed, his gaze on the paperwork in front of him. No doubt there was also information about the investigation in there.

"My father, uncle, and grandfather were all BPD."

"I haven't had the pleasure of meeting any of them," Breslin said. Kyler didn't respond, because the man's expression said he had something on his mind. Finally, the commissioner nailed him with a dark stare. "Given your long service here as well as that of your family, you're exactly the kind of officer we want on board. So I'd like you to tell me about the events that led up to your injuries this past May."

Kyler gave a tight nod. "I was attending the funeral of a friend's friend. The deceased was a criminal affiliated with the Church Gang, but I was there out of respect for his sister, who had only recently learned that. Some of the deceased's associates showed up, and a gunfight broke out." That was the shortest, sweetest version of the story Kyler could manage, so he shouldn't have been surprised when it wasn't enough. After all, you didn't get to be a police commissioner without having a finely tuned barometer for BS.

"Uh huh. Now tell me the rest of the story." The guy tilted his head, his expression calling bullshit on Vance's whitewashed version.

Problem was, Kyler was hamstrung in what he could say for a lot of reasons. The longer version was that Nick Rixey and some of his former Army Special Forces teammates were friends of Kyler's godfather, who'd been killed helping them investigate the conspiracies that'd gotten them ambushed in Afghanistan, ousted from the Army, and attacked by Baltimore's Church Gang, who was working with a handful of dirty military officials to smuggle and sell Afghani heroin. When Miguel had been killed, Kyler and his father had promised their assistance to Nick's team. It was what Miguel would've wanted. And Nick deserved the help, especially because the investigation he and Miguel had been running proved that the gang had a number of dirty cops in their pockets, too. But Kyler couldn't say all that. He couldn't admit that he'd essentially protected the team, hidden their investigation from the authorities, and helped cover up the real cause of the damage that had been done to the Rixeys' building. Because it would violate the nondisclosure agreements they'd all signed with the CIA, who'd come in at the very end to assist Nick and his team.

It was a fucking complicated mess.

So he said what he could. "This is all in my statements, sir. My godfather, Miguel Olivero, who'd been my father's partner, had called me in for some assistance with his private investigating business. Miguel was working a case that had something to do with the Church Gang and had gotten in over his head, especially when he identified some cops on the gang's payroll. Problem was, they cut him down before I learned all the details. I was in the middle of trying to figure it all out when the gunfight at the cemetery happened." This was the story Nick's CIA contact had helped Kyler devise. And Miguel wouldn't have minded one bit providing cover for Kyler this way. In fact, Ky could almost imagine Miguel chuckling up in Heaven and patting them all on the back for conceiving of such a good plan.

The thought set off a pang in Kyler's chest. He missed the old man like hell, and he knew his father did, too. Miguel had been a constant presence in both of the Vance men's lives. His loss left a big gaping hole that hadn't begun to close—and maybe never would.

"I read the statements, but I wanted you to look me in the eye when you recounted the story in your own words," Breslin said.

Damn, this guy was good. "And?"

"And…" The commissioner tilted his head, assessing him. "You're not telling me everything, but you don't strike me as dirty, either."

"I'm not dirty. And being lumped in with the pieces of shit responsible for Miguel's death is bullshit," Kyler said, meeting and holding his superior's observant gaze and reining in his mouth before it ran away with his career. Kyler was coming down on the side of Breslin being the real deal, and he wanted to earn the man's respect. And get out from behind that fucking desk.

Commissioner Breslin nodded. "Hang in there, Detective. I know this investigation is a burr on your balls, but we're moving as quickly as we can. I promise you that. And our methods will become clear soon enough."

Whatever that meant. But as he had no choice but to wait for the investigation to end, there was really only one thing for him to say. "Understood, sir."

"Good. Then we're done here, Detective. But my door is always open. Don't hesitate to use it." His boss gave him a pointed look, and Kyler nodded. "Dismissed."

Back at his desk again, Kyler forced himself to plow through some of the paperwork that buried the worn surface. The more he kept himself busy, the faster time would pass. But his mood was at least a little better than it had been earlier in the day. Because the more Kyler thought about it, the more positive his impressions of his conversation with the commissioner became. Without question, Breslin wasn't against him. And that counted for more than a little.

So Kyler would just keep his nose to the grindstone and make sure it stayed that way.

Chapter 5

The gallery opening was going even better than Mia had hoped. The place was packed. Buyers were opening their checkbooks. The four spotlighted artists were already pulling her aside to tell her how pleased they were. The arts editor from the city paper was here doing a story on the gallery. And Mia was currently sipping a glass of champagne that her boss, the gallery owner, had brought to her moments before with the words, "I knew you were the right person for this job."

Mia was on cloud nine.

"Girl, this is amazing," Dani said. She and a couple friends from DC had come up for the show, and Mia appreciated the support and the bodies. Nothing worse than an empty gallery on opening night. Not, it turned out, that she'd needed to worry.

"It really is, isn't it?" Mia said, a little stunned herself.

"Don't act so surprised. *You* made all this happen." Dani held up her glass and they clinked.

"I'm so glad you're here to share this with me," Mia said, squeezing her friend's hand. Dani was tall and athletic, with wavy, shoulder-length strawberry-blonde hair and pale blue eyes. The light and snarky to Mia's dark and more serious. They'd been fast friends from almost the moment they'd met in college.

"I wouldn't be anywhere else. You know this." Dani peered around them, then leaned in close. "So, when are you going back to see the blue-eyed orgasm machine?"

Mia nearly spit out her champagne. This is what spilling all the details got her. "Oh, my God, sshh," she whispered, unable to hold back from laughing. "I don't know. Maybe tomorrow. Though maybe I shouldn't, because he said he wasn't looking for a relationship."

"Dude, isn't that what all guys say?" Dani arched her eyebrow. The woman was a lawyer in a high-powered law firm and had been the managing editor of her law review, and she still said "dude" all the time. Mia loved it.

Shrugging, Mia managed to swallow the bubbly this time. "Maybe? I don't know."

"Isn't it win-win either way? You go and he plays again and you die of"—Dani's voice dropped to a whisper—"orgasmic bliss. Or you go and he doesn't want to play and you find someone else who's awesome? You said this club had more of the kind of men you like there than anywhere else you'd ever played, right?"

Mia nodded, peering around to make sure they weren't being overheard.

"I say you go," Dani said as if that settled it.

Mia was just about to respond when she spotted her father making his way through the crowd. She grinned. "My dad's here."

"There's my babydoll," he said when he made his way to her. He looked dashing in a dark blue pinstriped suit. They hugged.

"Hi, Daddy. I'm so glad you could come," she said. "You remember Dani."

"Of course," Dad said, giving Dani a quick hug. "Good to see you again, Dani."

"You, too. How's the new job?" Dani asked.

Her father shook his head and laughed. "Let's just say it's a challenge." He put his arm around Mia's shoulders. "But I'd say *your* job is going pretty damn good. Look at this turnout, Mia."

"I know. It's kinda crazy," she said, beaming under her dad's praise. He wasn't a man who gave compliments freely. You had to earn his respect, but once you had it, he was your fiercest ally and advocate. He'd always been both, for her, even after their parents divorced when she was twelve.

Mia still remembered overhearing the conversation that had been the beginning of their end. Her mother had told him she'd fallen out of love with him. And it'd broken Mia's heart on her dad's behalf. So she'd always made a special effort to stay in touch with him and visit him, even when her mother remarried. Her mom's husband was an amazing man, too, but her dad was her dad.

"It's not crazy," Dad said. "It's hard work paying off. I'm proud of you."

The rest of the night passed in a happy blur of introductions and networking and celebrating. It was the best, most fulfilling night of her professional life, and even though this show would be up for four weeks, the success of the night had her mind racing on all kinds of new ideas and plans for other events and shows.

Finally, everyone was gone, catering had cleaned up and left, and only Mia, her boss, Gregory Laponte, and Dani and her friends from DC remained.

"Go, get out of here," Gregory said, taking off his suit coat and rolling up his sleeves. A man of about sixty with a flare for fashion and an incredible eye for art, Gregory had made a name for himself as a philanthropist and a patron of the arts. This gallery was another of his pet projects—wanting to give up-and-coming artists in all kinds of media an opportunity to have their work seen and purchased by his impressive and extensive circle of friends. "You deserve a celebratory drink with your friends. I'll lock up."

"Are you sure? I don't mind taking care of everything," Mia said.

"I insist, sweetheart. You made me look mahvelous tonight. Go celebrate." He winked.

"Okay. See you soon," she said. He only came to the gallery a few times a week, so she didn't see him every day.

A few minutes later, she and the other girls spilled out onto the street and caught a cab to a fun wine bar down by the Inner Harbor. Mia was perfectly content hanging out and getting to know Dani's friends, but after just one drink, Dani said they should probably head out.

"Already?" Mia asked.

Her bestie gave her a pointed look, one that meant she was making it so that Mia was free to pursue *other* activities before the night was over. "Yeah. It's been a long day for you, and I need to bill some hours tomorrow anyway. Which means I should get home."

Mia said good-bye to everyone, and then she hugged Dani. "Thank you again, for everything."

"You're welcome, sweetie. I hope your night only gets better from here." Dani waggled her eyebrows.

Laughing, Mia waved as they caught a cab back to where they'd parked.

I'm not ready for the celebrating to be over, Mia thought. So she decided to take the gift that Dani had given her and run with it. She wasn't wearing play clothes, but the golden sheath cocktail dress she had on with the tall silver heels and the silver-and-gold jewelry was definitely upscale enough for Blasphemy. And anyway, she was hoping she wouldn't be wearing clothes for very long.

Annnd that was motivation enough to hail a cab of her own. Now she just hoped that Master Kyler was there, and that he was interested in playing, too.

* * * *

Kyler walked into Hard Ink Tattoo, ready for some new ink and to see some old friends. He hadn't known most of these guys for more than a few months, but after everything they'd been through together, it felt much longer. Sometimes it was just like that.

"Kyler Vance, how the hell are you?" Nick Rixey said, coming around the counter in the shop's reception area. Nick was former Army Special Forces, and in his build and the way he moved, you could still tell. Images of tattoo designs and finished ink covered the walls, and photo albums sat on a coffee table in front of an ugly old Naugahyde couch.

"Good, Nick. How's married life treating you?" Kyler asked.

Nick smiled, that single expression answering the question, and it reminded Kyler a whole helluva lot of how Isaac had looked the other night while texting with Willow. "I got no complaints," Nick said, running a hand through his dark hair, the smile extending to his odd, pale green eyes. "Jeremy's finishing up with his client, but come on back. Everyone's hanging in the lounge."

Down a narrow hall, they passed a series of tattoo rooms on either side, and then the space opened up into a big square lounge. Tables filled the center, and a grouping of couches took up one corner. On the back wall, a large graffiti-like mural read, "Bleed with me, and you'll forever be my brother." It struck a chord with Kyler every time he saw it. He had bled with these guys. It bonded you in ways not everyone could understand.

A big chorus of greetings rang out when everyone saw him, and soon Kyler was shaking the men's hands and hugging all the women. After their investigations were finally resolved back in May, Nick and his former teammates had agreed to form a security consulting company, and now they all lived here and worked together—Shane McCallan, the team's medic, Edward "Easy" Cantrell, an explosives specialist, Derek "Marz" DiMarzio, a genius in all things computer, and Beckett Murda, a man who could build or improve pretty much any gadget. Jeremy's boyfriend, Charlie Merritt, was also there, the guy as brilliant as Marz on the computer. Together, they were a formidable team, as their success against truly stunning odds attested.

"We were wondering when we were gonna get to see you again," Becca Rixey said, her arm looped through Nick's. She was girl-next-door pretty and an ER nurse who'd proven fantastic in a crisis. And these guys had had more than a few. "I'm so glad you came over."

"Me, too," Kyler said.

"How's your arm doing?" Kat asked. Nick's sister had the trademark Rixey look, with her chocolate-brown hair and green eyes, but she was much shorter than either of her brothers. And since she'd been shot at the cemetery, too—in the chest, Kyler didn't mind the question coming from her.

"I'm almost a hundred percent again. How about you? You look great," Kyler said, standing in the midst of this big circle of friends. He really did need to come hang more often. Especially while all this bullshit with the IA investigation was going on. Being in his head didn't do him any good.

"I feel great, actually. Really good." She grinned up at Beckett, standing right behind her, and the softness in his expression when he looked at her was striking given what a hardass he normally was.

"Some might even say she was *glowing*," Marz said dramatically as he made a funny face and nodded toward her.

Kyler looked between Kat and Beckett's best friend. "Wait, are you pregnant?" he asked Kat.

"Geez, D. You'd think you were the father," Shane said, humor bringing out the guy's southern accent. Everyone laughed.

"What? I'm the proud uncle. I can't help it," Marz said, holding out his hands.

"Well, damn. Congratulations to you both." Kyler shook Beckett's hand and hugged Kat again. And it struck him—if they hadn't been successful at uncovering the conspiracy against the team, Kat and Beckett wouldn't have this incredible thing happening right now, this little life they'd made together. And that…that made everything Kyler had been going through these past couple of months suddenly feel even more worthwhile than he'd thought. Damn. Life was funny sometimes.

"Dude, I'm ready for you," Jeremy said, coming up to join the circle. Kyler shook his tattooed hand.

"Yeah? I'm just getting caught up on all the good news out here," Kyler said, taking Jeremy in. The guy had already looked much better at Becca and Nick's wedding than he had earlier in the summer, but now you'd almost never know that a few months ago he'd had brain surgery. Now he was just the Jeremy that Kyler had first met—covered in tattoos, piercings in his face, and always a smile, a joke, or a kind word to share. Kyler's gaze dropped to Jeremy's T-shirt, which read, *I would do me*. Grinning, Kyler pointed. "Nice one."

"Right?" Jeremy said, winking. His T-shirt collection was apparently famous. Or infamous. Kyler wasn't sure which.

"Well, since numb-nuts shared my good news, I might as well share that he and Emilie are engaged," Beckett said, smirking at Marz.

But Marz just looked proud, as in grinning-like-an-idiot proud. The guy put his arm around Emilie Garza, the woman whose brother had been buried at the cemetery that day. "She agreed to marry me and all my legs. So that makes her a keeper in my book," he said. Another round of laughter, and Kyler had to respect him for making peace the way he had with the amputation he'd suffered in the ambush that had ended their military careers.

"Clearly, I can't stay away so long next time," Kyler said as he offered more congratulations. "I need to come bask in all your good news."

"And there will be more to come. Just you wait," Becca said, smiling up at Nick.

Kyler almost hated to leave the group, but he also knew that Jeremy was working past closing time, and he didn't want to hold the man up anymore than he was already doing. In Jer's tattoo room, Kyler took a seat and explained what he wanted. Within a few minutes, Jeremy had drawn it on a sheet of tracing paper.

"That's it," Kyler said, turning to sit backward on the chair so Jeremy could get to his shoulder. "Exactly. Do it."

For the next ninety minutes, Jeremy worked on him, inking a tribal cross with pointed ends onto the back of his right shoulder. The design featured a thick black outline the whole way around, and a dark blue line that filled the center. It was for Miguel. Jeremy had added some tribal blades behind the cross, and Kyler already knew it was going to be a piece he would cherish.

"All done," Jeremy finally said. "Take a look."

Grasping a hand mirror, Kyler stepped to the wall mirror and examined the new ink on his shoulder. "Well fucking done, Jeremy. For real." The piece was about six inches tall, the dark colors bold against his skin.

"Glad you like. Let me bandage you up and you'll be good to go."

Kyler dropped back in the chair so Jer could finish. "So, do you have good news to share, too?"

"Shop's open again, which is awesome. The other half of the building has a finished shell, which is ahead of schedule. And I have the most amazing boyfriend in the world. That might be as much good as I can take at one time," he said, chuckling.

"That's a lot," Kyler said. "Good for you." Kyler meant it, too. Even though all these happy couples at Hard Ink emphasized his solitude a whole helluva lot, didn't they?

When it was time, Jeremy refused to take his money. "Your money's no good here, Vance. But I'm your guy. Any time. Any ink you want. Come to me." Jer held out his hand.

"I'll find another way to repay you," Kyler said. "But you can believe I'll be back for more work."

"Good. You better be," Jeremy said, his tongue flicking at the piercing on his lip.

Kyler said his good-byes to the last members of the group still hanging out in the lounge, and then he was back out into the night. It was late—after eleven o'clock—but he wasn't ready to go home. Seeing his friends had made him feel energized, and getting the tattoo had adrenaline flowing through his system.

He wanted to go to Blasphemy. But he really didn't want to see Mia. Not tonight. Tonight, he didn't want a reminder of something else he couldn't have. So he called the control room at the club.

"Yo, Kyler. What can I do for you?" Zeke asked. They rotated the jobs they did around the club.

"Hey, Z. A new submissive named Mia joined on Wednesday night. Any idea if she's checked in tonight?" Kyler asked.

"Hold on," Zeke said. Then, "No. I don't see anyone by that name."

The relief Kyler expected didn't come. Instead, there was just an odd resignation. "Good deal. Thanks, man." They hung up.

But at least it meant that he was in the clear to go there and not break his rules. Because he was in the mood to play.

Chapter 6

Mia had only been at Blasphemy for ten minutes, but she already knew that Kyler wasn't there. First she'd looked, and then she'd just come out and asked the dark-blond-haired man named Master Leo who was bartending tonight. For a moment, she'd been struck by the fact that the Dom had two different-colored eyes—one blue, the other green. But then he said that it wasn't Master Kyler's night to work, apparently, and he hadn't come in to hang out as he apparently had the other night.

She wasn't sure what she wanted to do. Did she potentially want to play with someone else? Did she want to wait? Or did she want to go home?

Her belly squeezed at that last one. She didn't want to go home. This was her big night. She wanted to celebrate somehow. Besides, Master Kyler had been explicit that he wasn't interested in a relationship, so maybe he wouldn't want to play with her again anyway. Mia sighed. Maybe she'd just have a look around.

As she walked from one public scene to the other, she caught a lot of looks, and not a few compliments, because of her dress. Form-fitting and strapless, she really loved the brightness of the gold color against her skin, the way the ruching on the skirt emphasized her curves, and the beading on the bodice that sparkled and shined. She felt elegant and refined, and that had been perfect for earlier in the night. But now she kinda wanted someone to mess her up and take her apart.

Up on what had once been the church's altar, a bondage scene was taking place in front of a rapt audience. Mia's mouth dropped open because she recognized the black-haired Dom—Master Griffin, who had...the most fascinating tattoo that she'd ever seen. It covered his entire back in blacks and reds. A woman's face, partially obscured by her dark hair whipping in front of her features as if blown by the wind, streaks of red framing the image. It spoke to the artist in Mia, even though it made her wonder who the woman was and whether she had anything to do with the fact that when the Dom smiled, it didn't really reach his eyes.

Stepping closer, she watched Master Griffin work a flogger over the bound woman's body, admiring the beauty of what he'd wrought in bright blue rope. The submissive hung on her side from a circular hook, ropes securing her top leg straight up, her bottom leg bent back—her thighs wide, and her upper body with her arms behind her back. The Dom was apparently skilled at a Japanese style of rope bondage called Shibari, known for the beautiful patterns the arrangement of the ropes and knots made on the submissive's body. Because the scene before her was as beautiful as it was erotic. Mia had never had it done, but watching him work made her want to try it. At least once.

"As intriguing as this scene is, it's hard to look anywhere else but at you in that stunning dress," a male voice said from behind her.

Mia turned toward the Dom and smiled. "Thank you, Sir." No wrist cuff, so he wasn't one of the Masters. He was attractive, with silvering hair and brown eyes.

"I'm Richard," he said, holding out his hand.

"Hello," she said, shaking his hand. "I'm Mia."

"Have you seen Master Griffin work before?" he asked, gesturing at the stage. "He is better at Shibari than anyone here."

Mia turned her gaze back to the scene. "No, I'm pretty new. But the rope work is gorgeous on her," she said, looking back to him. And that was when, out of the corner of her eye, she spotted Kyler. She smiled at him, sure that he'd seen her, but he turned away. "Excuse me, Sir. I see a friend I was hoping to catch up with tonight."

"Lucky friend," he said. "Of course."

Mia made her way through the back of the audience, but by the time she'd made it to where Master Kyler had been, he was gone. It was much busier in here for being Friday night, so it made looking for him harder to do. Finally, she went to the bar, which was where he'd found her that first night. She waited, and Master Leo confirmed that she hadn't just imagined Kyler's presence when he volunteered that he'd showed after all.

Was he avoiding her? Maybe their time together hadn't been as mind-blowing for him as it had been for her. Because her mind had definitely been blown. The way he'd handled her, the words that spilled from his mouth, his fearlessness in giving her what she needed. And if that hadn't all been enough, the way he'd cared for her after had really made her regret that he didn't want a relationship, because the way he'd treated her could definitely tempt her heart to enter into the equation.

She peered around for him again. No luck.

He was here. He'd seen her. And he wasn't coming for her. And Master Kyler struck her as a man who knew what he wanted and took it. Damn.

Part of her really wanted to go home. To go wallow in the disappointment welling up in her belly. But if she did that, she was just going to end up thinking about Master Kyler anyway.

Not to mention, she only had this discounted membership for another eleven days. She didn't want to miss out on that, because she wasn't sure whether she'd be able to afford continuing it at the regular rate, and she didn't have a Dom who would pay it for her.

Mia debated, Blasphemy's vibe appealing to something deep inside her. She wasn't leaving. Richard had seemed nice. Maybe she could talk to him again. Or maybe she could find someone else. Either way, there was no sense in waiting for Kyler. That much seemed clear.

And a half hour of being here—of watching the bondage scene and so much else—had aroused her. She didn't want to leave on that account, either. Mia needed this.

That resolved her. She slipped off the stool and resumed her explorations. The bondage scene was over, and Master Griffin was wrapping the submissive in a blanket in a way that tugged at something deep inside Mia. Turning away, she joined the crowd gathered around the St. Andrew's cross, a woman strapped to it and a different Master working over her skin with a flogger until she was pink almost everywhere.

A thrill shot through Mia.

And then her arousal ratcheted higher. Because the Dom traded out his flogger for a vibrating massager and held it against her clit while he clamped his hand around the submissive's throat. The woman came twice almost immediately, and Mia was close to coming just from watching, just *imagining* that it was happening to her.

"Hey, new girl," came a deep voice as someone stepped in beside her.

"Master Quinton," Mia said with a smile. "I'm not new anymore, don't you know? I'm an old pro now."

He laughed, and the deepness of the chuckle was so sexy.

"You here to play tonight, or are you just taking things in?" His expression was interested, and Mia's stomach flipped. Because Master Quinton was hot and funny and *big*.

"I was hoping to play," she said, meeting his gaze.

"You interested in learning my other superpowers?" He grinned, his expression full of a playful smugness.

She laughed. "Maybe I am."

"Come with me. Let's talk," he said, taking her hand. He led her toward the same side of the nave that Kyler had, but instead of turning down the hallway to the little nook with the couch, he led her across it. And the fact that she couldn't look at that couch—that she feared that she'd be reminded of her time with Master Kyler or, worse, see him there *now* with someone else—told her that maybe she wasn't in the right frame of mind to please Master Quinton the way she should. Disappointment slinking through her, she inhaled to fess up.

"Master Quinton?" came a man's voice. And not just any man.

The big Dom beside her turned. "Master Kyler. I didn't know you were in tonight." The men shook hands.

"Yeah," Master Kyler said, his gaze finally landing on Mia. His eyes were totally on fire, but she couldn't tell if it was passion or anger that had him so wound up. Awkwardness settled between the three of them until Mia's face was hot. She ducked her chin.

"You know," Master Quinton said, dragging a hand through his light brown hair. "I just remembered a thing. I'm very sorry, Mia. Please accept my apologies." He kissed her on the cheek.

"Of course, Sir," she said.

Master Quinton clapped Kyler on the shoulder. "See ya later, man."

And then it was just her and a kinda pissed-off looking Master Kyler. He wore angry well. As in, the harshness of the set of his jaw and the tight press of his lips and the narrow cut of his eyes—they were all hot, especially coming from a Dom. But she didn't understand it.

"Um. Hello, Sir," she finally said when he didn't say anything.

"Mia," he said, his gaze raking over her. "You look absolutely stunning tonight." His voice was like gravel, rough and strained.

"Thank you. Are you okay, Sir?" she asked.

He shook his head. "I don't...I don't know."

"Do you want to sit and talk?" Mia asked, concern for him flooding her.

Suddenly, Kyler pinned her to the cool wall. He braced his hands on either side of her head, and he was erect against her belly. She wanted to drop into a crouch and take him into her mouth. "Do you want vulgar honesty or watered-down politeness?" he asked.

The promise of those words made her core clench with need. "Vulgar honesty."

He nailed her with a blue-eyed stare. "I don't want to sit and talk. I want to fuck. Hard. I want to be aggressive. Maybe I even want to be a little mean."

Mia's heart was suddenly a runaway train in her chest. Because, sign her up! She let out a shaky breath. "That sounds...like someone's going to have a good night," she managed.

Kyler dropped his head to her shoulder on a groan. He knocked his forehead against the bone there once, twice.

"Did I say the wrong thing?" she asked. Because he was totally confusing her.

"That's just it, Mia. I don't know." He lifted his gaze to hers again.

"How can I help?" she asked.

For a moment, he closed his eyes and inhaled deeply, and when he opened them, it was like he'd centered himself and made some kind of resolution. "Are you game for what I just described?" He fingered the chunky silver-and-gold choker she wore around her neck.

Heat swept over her, her body already answering, already preparing. "Yes, Sir. I am."

He gave a tight nod and backed up a step. "Let me show you the room I have in mind." Taking her hand, he led her down the long hallway that shot off the side of the nave. She wasn't sure if this was still part of the church building or something else, but she didn't have long to wonder before Kyler stopped at a door and keyed in a code.

Lights came on as the door opened, and Kyler guided her inside with his hand at the small of her back.

Just the room's theme turned her on. Concrete floor. Cinder-block walls with peeling paint. Light thrown from bare lightbulbs surrounded by little cages. An iron cot bed with only a white fitted sheet. Rusted metal cabinet at the side that undoubtedly held a variety of toys and supplies. It looked like a basement or a warehouse—a place where a woman in a beautiful cocktail dress had no business being. A role started taking shape in her mind.

"Do you see where my head is tonight, Mia?" Master Kyler asked, his body almost rigid with tension.

God, she was going to enjoy helping him work out whatever had him so wound up. "Yes, Sir."

He stood right in front of her, his gaze intent, assessing. The dark blue button down he wore brought out the blue of his eyes even more. "How do you feel about role-playing a non-consensual scene?"

Heat roared over her body. She'd wanted someone to mess up her elegant persona. *This*. This was exactly what she wanted tonight. Something dark and dirty and hot for being both. She felt her pulse kick up against her skin. Everywhere. "I'm okay with that, Sir."

His eyes narrowed. "Just okay?" He stroked his knuckles down her cheek.

"No. More. Um, I'm definitely interested. I want it, Master Kyler."

His calloused hand gently cupped her cheek and pulled her to him. His lips fell on hers, tender and sensual. He kissed her lazily, tugging her lips with his and slowly exploring her mouth with his tongue. He tasted like whiskey and sin, and she wasn't sure which was more intoxicating.

He pulled back but kept their faces close. His thumb stroked the apple of her cheek. "You really do look beautiful."

"Thank you," she whispered, warmth spreading through her.

"How did your big gallery opening go?" he asked.

"How did you remember that?" Surprise and excitement unleashed a funny, happy feeling in her chest.

"Because it was important to you," he said, simply.

Six words. Six words that could easily own her. "It went amazingly. A total success." She couldn't help the smile that accompanied the words.

"Good for you," he said, kissing her forehead. "Congratulations."

"Thank you, Sir," she said. Gah! Why didn't this man want a relationship?

"I was angry before, Mia, but I want you to know that I'm not now. I'm in control."

Mia didn't need him to say that. Unlike in the hallway, he exuded a calm confidence now, his shoulders relaxed, his face at ease, his eyes communicating only passion. She grasped his hand where it still held her face and pulled it to her mouth. She kissed the back of his hand. His knuckles. His fingers. "I know, Sir."

Master Kyler swallowed hard, the sound thick. His eyes were trained on her mouth against his hand. "Jesus," he whispered under his breath. Finally, he squeezed her hand and pulled away, the smile playing around his mouth making it clear he wasn't displeased. "Are you ready to play, Mia?"

Her belly flipped at the dark, heady promise of what was about to happen. "Yes, Sir."

"Then take off your dress so it doesn't get torn. Leave everything else on and kneel on one end of the bed, your back to the headboard. When I say 'Scene,' we begin."

Chapter 7

Kyler had tried to stay away from her. When he'd seen her across the club, he'd walked away. Despite the fact that her dress made him want to unwrap her, that the updo of her lovely brown hair bared that beautiful throat, and that his body was making demands of him that his brain didn't want to answer.

And then she'd made it worse. First, by walking away from the Dom who was clearly interested in her. Second, by waiting at the bar—for Kyler—he had no doubt that's what she'd been doing. And third by finally giving up on Kyler, and then finding a possible replacement in Master Quinton.

When Quinton had taken her hand—had touched what Kyler's body screamed was *his*—Kyler hadn't been able to stay away anymore.

And now, here they were. Kyler in a dark mood. And Mia seemingly all the more turned on for it. It was almost like she knew what he needed her to be, or do, to ease him. And that felt like a really fucking dangerous thing.

That danger didn't have him walking out of the room though, did it?

No, instead, he was tying her to the bed. She was kneeling with her legs spread wide, which allowed Kyler to secure her hands and ankles behind her using rope tied to the iron. She could only lean so far forward before the rope would catch her. He tied another rope around her waist, with loops around each of her upper thighs, and attached that one to the almost equally high footboard—this rope would not only keep her from leaning back, but it would keep her from being able to sag down onto her calves. The two sets of ropes largely immobilized her so that she had to take whatever he did. After he arranged everything else he needed, he turned to her.

"What are your safe words?" he asked. She gave him the right answers. "And if you're gagged?"

Mia shook her head three times while humming, "Mmm, mmm, mmm."

"Very good, Mia. Are there any words or names you don't like to be called while role-playing?"

"No, Sir," she said, her voice so aroused that he could've thrown her down and skipped all the buildup.

But she deserved better than that. He nailed her with a long look, giving her—and himself—one last chance. But they were doing this. "Scene." Grabbing the medical scissors and a strap, he approached her, his persona shifting to fit the role he had in mind. "Well, what do we have here?"

"Please, let me go," she said, her big brown eyes pleading as she struggled against the ropes.

Kyler pulled off his T-shirt and tossed it aside, ignoring the burn under the gauze from his new tattoo. "I don't think that's in the cards for you." He moved behind her, enjoying her begging for one more moment.

"Please. I have money. I could pay you a reward," she said, her voice desperate.

That she was embracing this scene drove arousal and satisfaction through him in equal measure. "Your money's not what I want," he growled. He gagged her with the leather strap and secured it behind her head. "Make all the noise you want. No one can hear you."

He came around and leaned on the bed in front of her, his gaze drinking her in. The strapless bra and panties she wore were a shimmery gold set, beautiful against her skin. He'd replace them.

"Don't think you'll be needing these," he said. As she moaned and tried to get away, he placed the scissors at the piece of satin between her breasts and cut off her bra.

Mia cried out around the gag and tried to pull away from him, but the ropes held her steady. He smacked one breast, then the other, repeating it until the generous mounds were pink and Mia was moaning.

He dragged his fingers over her nipples, squeezing and pinching, and then down to the crotch of her panties. They were already wet. Fuck. "What a slut you are. I knew you wanted this."

She moaned and thrashed. Kyler removed her panties with slow cuts at each hipbone. He dipped his hand between her legs. Just fucking drenched. He had to bite back a groan. Because she was totally going there on this with him, and it was turning her on as much as him. He sank a finger deep. "Ever had a felon inside you before?" he asked, looking up at her.

Garbled words that sounded like, "Please, no."

Kyler chuckled. "Bet you wanted one, though. Huh? Someone to give you a real down-and-dirty fuck. Not the polite, boring fucks I bet you get. That's why you're here, right?" He added a second and finger-fucked her, the heel of his palm hitting and grinding on her clit.

Mia moaned and tried to tilt her hips into his touch. "Please," she said.

"I like when you beg me." He pumped into her harder. "Do it again."

The whine she released went straight to his cock. Because it sounded like she was as tightly wound as he was. After a few more pumps, he moved behind her and unlatched the heavy chain necklace she wore. He'd been jealous of this fucking piece of jewelry since he first saw her because it looked too damn much like a public collar. And if she was going to have something around her neck, it was going to be something he put there. Damnit. He pulled the black animal collar from his pocket and held it up in front of her. "This is more your style now."

She shook her head as he secured it, and when she kept thrashing, he grabbed her by the throat. Squeezed. Lifted.

He got right in her face. "You better do as I fucking say. You want to make me happy, right?"

Pleading, lust-filled eyes peered up at him. "Yes, yes, yes," she said around the gag.

"Yeah, I thought so." He released his grip and she gasped in air. "And you can do that by coming. Again and again. To show me how hot you are to be here." He grabbed the Hitachi wand, knelt next to her leg, and placed its vibrating head in his palm. Leaning over the narrow cot so he was in front of her, he held it right up to her clit, his fingers between her legs. He sank his middle and fourth fingers into her pussy so he could stimulate her G-spot, too.

Mia screamed and threw her head back.

"That close already, huh?" Moving his fingers inside her, he ground the vibrations harder against her clit.

"Oh, God," she moaned.

He worked his fingers harder. "Show me you like this, slut."

"No, no, no," she cried.

"Do it. Do it, *now*."

Mia came magnificently. Her whole body went taut and she screamed around the strap, her orgasm wetting his fingers and spilling onto his palm. And then she did it again. And again. Until he thought she might pass out and he might come just from the exquisite fucking beauty of her pleasure.

He removed the wand and tossed it aside on the bed. Putting his face in her line of sight, he licked at his wet fingers. Salty and sweet. "I'm gonna enjoy you." Kyler wiped a streak of wetness over her lips.

Quickly, he untied the ropes from the bed. Manhandling Mia, he turned her around, still on her knees. She struggled against him, her hands striking at his chest, making Kyler smile.

"I like it when you fight me, but you aren't going to win. Hands on the headboard," he growled. When her movements weren't fast enough, he slapped her luscious ass. "Now."

She gripped the iron, and he tied her hands in place. Next, he positioned a spreader bar between her knees, forcing her legs wide.

"Please, please just let me go," she cried, her words garbled.

"Oh, little Mia, you're mine now. I'm never letting you go," Kyler said, the words coming from the character he was playing. But then he paused mid-movement, because the sentiment reached inside his chest and poked at things he never messed with—his solitude, his loneliness, his jealousies of what others had that he never would. In a quick flash, his memory conjured the happiness on the faces of Nick and Becca, Beckett and Kat, Marz and Emilie.

Fuck.

Fuck.

Why did this woman get to him this way?

Standing beside the bed behind her, Kyler's gaze ran over Mia's bound form. Her curvy body appealed to everything male inside him. Her need for darker, edgier sexual activities matched his so well. Her laughter lit him up inside. And the fact that she'd asked if he was okay and kissed his knuckles revealed that she could read him, too.

If he was the kind of man who did relationships, she was the kind of woman he'd want.

But what he had was this moment. *All* he had was this moment.

Get out of your fucking head, Vance.

Kyler grabbed the flogger from the cabinet and ran its soft leather straps over his hand. He'd seen Mia's face as she watched the flogging scene. She'd liked it.

He got on the bed behind her, and Mia gasped as the cot jostled.

With four quick turns of his wrist, he brought the flogger down over her back. She moaned and sagged against the headboard. Kyler worked her ass over next. He ducked his hand between her legs and penetrated with a finger. Her wet pussy sucked at him. Three quick flicks against one ass cheek. Her core sucked harder. "Mmm. Someone likes a little pain with fucking, doesn't she?"

"Nonono," she moaned, thrashing as much as she could. Which wasn't much.

"Liar. Don't lie to me, slut. Your body sure doesn't," Kyler said, finger-fucking her hard and fast for a moment. She arched her back for more. He gave it to her until her whole backside was pink and warm and she was moaning nonstop, her endorphins probably flying.

Kyler couldn't hold back any longer. Smearing her wetness over her ass cheek, he dropped the flogger and undid his jeans. Shoved them to his knees. Quickly rolled on a condom.

And then he was right up against her, his chest to her back, her front to the cold, unforgiving iron.

Kyler took his cock in hand and guided it to her pussy. And then he shoved deep in one mind-blowing stroke. "*Fuuck*," he groaned.

Mia's moan matched his in intensity and need.

"Knew you needed this," he said. *Needed me*, his mind offered. Which proved just how fucked he was over this woman, didn't it? He shouldn't want her to need him. "Say it," he growled. "Tell me."

"Needed it, needed it, yes," she said, her words a fast, mumbled rush. She ground her ass backward into him, shoving him deeper.

He withdrew slowly and penetrated again in a series of hard, punctuated thrusts. "Don't. Fucking. Forget it." He pulled her hips back, forcing her to bend at the waist. And then Kyler rode her like a man possessed. Fast. Hard. Merciless. He might've worried about the pace and intensity except her pussy was already fisting his cock, tighter, tighter.

Testing what she'd said the other night, he grabbed the back of the collar around her throat and twisted it, increasing the pressure a little at first. Then a lot more.

Mia shrieked. And then she came and came, her juices wetting them both.

Kyler groaned at the fucking perfection of it. And knew that his need was too urgent to drag this out the way he really wanted.

Hunching his body over hers, giving her his weight, he gripped both hands around her throat like he was strangling her from behind. Using the leverage of his hold there, he pounded into her, and *goddamn hell*, she came again, her body bowing so hard that she lifted him with the arch of her spine.

It was the nail in the coffin of his restraint.

"Too good, Mia. Christ, it's too good." He came on a shout, his hips grinding into her, his cock jerking hard inside her, his body riding a high unlike anything he'd felt in a long, long time. Maybe ever.

When he finally calmed, he pressed kisses all down Mia's shoulder.

"Hang on a sec, Mia, and I'll get you untied." He removed the strap from her mouth and stroked a hand over her soft hair, not as neat as it had been earlier. Kyler disposed of the condom and did up his jeans. Removed the spreader bar. Unbound her hands. Massaged where the ropes had made impressions in her skin.

She sagged, her muscles lax.

"Look at me," he said. She did, though her gaze was a little unfocused. "Tell me how you are." He recalled how much she'd dropped the last time, and he hadn't dealt out nearly the amount of pain play then that he had tonight.

"I'm good, Sir," she said, her voice soft.

Kyler covered her with a blanket, tucking it around her shoulders. "Just rest there a minute." He made quick work of cleaning up the room. When everything was put away, he returned to her. "Come here, little one," he said. She shifted toward him, her movements slow, and Kyler lifted her into his arms.

Mia tucked herself against his bare chest on a long, satisfied sigh. And it fucking owned him. It really did.

A door on the room's rear wall opened into a small private lounge with an overstuffed couch, table, and a shelf full of supplies. A tray with drinks and snacks sat on the table, the same as he'd ordered the other night after his first scene with Mia. Quinton. Kyler would've put money on it. He couldn't decide whether to be chagrined or annoyed at the other Dom's knowing what they'd need, but Mia was all that mattered just then.

He sat with Mia in his lap, all her soft curves comforting him, *easing* him. An hour with her and every bit of the day's agitation was gone. Comfort and ease. How fucking rare for him these past months. Ever since the horror of seeing Miguel's gunned-down body discarded on the street like so much trash, Kyler had been living a nightmare that just wouldn't end. Now, because of Mia, comfort and ease. She'd given him so much that he could've fallen asleep with her. Right there on that couch.

"Drink," he said, handing her a water.

She did, slow sips turning into gulps. When she was done, she heaved a deep breath.

"How are you doing?" he asked, his fingers stroking her cheek. He examined her neck for marks, but her skin was clear.

"Good. I feel…good. A little drunk. Kinda like I'm not quite in my skin," she said, some of the words almost slurred. She peered up at him with soft, fuzzy, sated eyes.

Damn, Mia could really get deep into subspace. Would another Dom know that about her? Know that her ability to detach meant he had to take extra care to monitor her pain and reactions? Know she needed extra attention, especially after an intense scene? A rock settled into his gut.

"Are you okay?" she asked.

"Me. Yes. Why do you ask?"

"Your shoulder is bandaged," she said, her brow furrowing.

Her concern touched him. "Don't worry. It's just a new tattoo."

"Oh." Her gaze dropped to the front of his right shoulder, and he answered her question before she asked.

"The scars are from surgery. A few months ago." He didn't see the need to add that he'd been shot, which would only open up a whole other complicated conversation. And right now what he needed was a break from work, not to discuss it. "Are you uncomfortable with anything that happened, Mia?" he asked, hoping he hadn't pushed her beyond where she wanted to go.

She shook her head. "It was…good. Hot. I've always wanted to do something like that." She smiled, then pressed a soft kiss to his cheek. "Thank you, Master."

The word reached into his chest…reached into his chest and grabbed ahold. Master. He should correct her because he wasn't her Master. He wasn't. But *fuck*. Part of him wanted to be. Bad.

How had that happened so quickly? How had that happened *at all*?

Because he'd never let it happen before.

Sonofabitch.

Mia yawned, then chuckled. "Sorry."

"Don't be. Rest on me, Mia. I've got you," Kyler said, cradling her head against his shoulder. She fell asleep almost immediately. And as unconsciousness called to Kyler, too, his last thought was, *Yeah, but how long can I really let myself keep her?*

Chapter 8

With so few days until her temporary membership expired, Mia hadn't been able stay away from Blasphemy. She'd work all day and find herself at the club as many nights as her schedule and other commitments allowed.

The third time she'd come, she'd met Master Kyler manning the reception area. He'd found her after his shift was done, and they'd played. He'd hogtied her on a bed. Lying on her stomach, he secured her arms and legs to a spreader bar behind her, forcing her whole body to arch back. And then he'd made it worse by tying a leather strap around her neck and securing that to the bar, too. If she relaxed to take the pressure off her back, the strap choked her tighter. Which was the point. He'd made her come a half dozen times with a vibrator, and she'd been so deliciously delirious that they hadn't had sex. But she hadn't minded that so much when he'd told her when he'd be at the club again.

And she'd reveled in the faint bruises on her throat that had required her to wear one of her many scarves the next few days.

Each time was hotter than the next.

There was the time he'd had her straddle a Sybian machine, a hump-shaped toy with a dildo and vibrating pad that ground into her clit, and fucked her face so hard and so deep that she was gagging and gasping for air and coming so many times he had to hold her upright to finish. They hadn't had sex that night, either. But then there was the time they'd been watching Master Griffin doing another Shibari demonstration on the church's altar, and she'd gotten turned on. So Master Kyler had taken her from behind right there, in the middle of the crowd, his hand alternating between grasping her throat and smothering her mouth and nose. And the breath play along with having so many people watching—from so close—had made her squirt so hard she'd pushed him out of her.

After they'd play, he'd hold her and soothe her, and each time he'd let her know when he was going to be there again. She couldn't help but hold out a little hope that meant something, even though he'd been very clear on more than one occasion.

Now, on the last night of her temporary membership, Mia found herself once again in Master Kyler's arms after an incredibly intense and hot scene, this one based entirely around orgasm denial.

He'd strapped her to a table in the medical-themed room, her legs bound in adjustable stirrups. And then he experimented on her body with different implements, tools, and forms of torment to see what got her the hottest the fastest—and then he denied her release at the last moment. Over and over again. If that hadn't been sensual torture enough, the medical room had a big window with audience seating, and they'd drawn a crowd who watched as Master Kyler tormented her so exquisitely. She'd cursed his name through the first two-thirds of it, but when he finally allowed her to do so, she came so hard so many times that she forgot her own damn name.

The audience had cheered.

It had been their sixth scene together, and she was utterly addicted to this man. To everything about him.

Now, lying in Master Kyler's lap in a little private lounge, she wasn't sure if she still had any bones in her body.

Unfortunately, her mind wasn't nearly as peaceful as her satisfied body should've allowed. Because tonight was her last night. From here, the club would evaluate her time so far and offer her a full membership, assuming a current member recommended her. And then she'd have to pay the regular rate.

She just didn't see how she could afford it.

Which either meant that tonight was the last night she'd ever see Master Kyler…or that she had to be brave enough to ask to see him outside of the club. And *that* was a damn scary proposition since he'd explicitly told her he didn't want a relationship.

Even though, for someone who didn't want one, he was really freaking good at making her feel cared for. And that caring—from the way he read her needs in a scene to the way he'd asked about her gallery opening to the way he'd let her fall asleep on him on more than one occasion—it was all pulling her emotions into the equation. She didn't just like Master Kyler. Or lust after him. She wanted him—wanted *more* with him. Maybe even wanted to be his.

Kyler's fingers stroked over her hair, the feeling luring her eyes to close. If only her brain would stop racing. "What are you thinking so hard about, little one?" Lazy, male satisfaction made his tone deep, graveled.

Maybe she should just lay part of this out there and see where he went with it. "Tonight's my last night."

Underneath her, his muscles tensed. "What do you mean?" He tilted her chin so that they looked at each other.

"My membership." She gave a little shrug. "It was one of the temporary ones. It ends tonight."

His gorgeous face was a careful neutral. Her belly waited...waited...and then started a slow sinking. "Your membership was..." He shook his head. "Will you go for the full membership?"

Did that mean he wanted her to? "I'm not sure. To be honest, it would be a stretch for me financially."

"I see," he said, his gaze searching hers and losing some of its warmth in the process. Or maybe that was her imagination? Or her heartache?

She hung on his words, hoping he'd say something more. Needing him to.

"Well, I...I hope it works out." His brow furrowed for just a moment.

He hoped...it worked out? What the hell did *that* mean? Master Kyler was a Dom who knew exactly how to say what he wanted. Clearly and without any pretense. That vague mess of words right there? Well, it told her everything she didn't want to know, didn't it?

Suddenly, she needed off of his lap, out of his arms, away from him. How had she let herself want more when he'd told her he couldn't give it? Or wouldn't. So, so dumb. But she just nodded. "Thank you for everything, Master Kyler. I'm going to head out." She shifted.

He caught her around the waist, and she bit back a whimper. Because she really needed to get away from him—before she lost her temper or started to cry. Both reactions were bubbling up inside her. She pushed against his chest.

"Wait," he said.

The word nearly made her gasp as hope rushed through her. "Why?" she asked, her voice strained. She forced herself to meet his gaze. But she didn't find hope there.

"You're…are you feeling okay again? After the scene, I mean?" He frowned.

Oh. She'd never achieved the depth of subspace with another Dom that she did with him, so she'd never experienced the fuzzy-headed euphoria and emotional roller coaster that it could take you on after a scene. They'd talked about that a bit after they'd fallen asleep together the first time, the night he'd first showed her his amazing cross tattoo. Just one more thing she liked about him, the sexy ink covering so much of his body. He'd said he was worried about her going into subspace with a less experienced Dominant and suggested she advise any future Doms before she played with them about how pain and intensity could impact her.

At the time, she'd just thought he was looking out for her.

But now… If his words tonight didn't quash the stupid, stupid hope she'd momentarily felt, the memory of that exchange stomped on it with a pair of big, beefy shitkickers. "I'm fine, Sir. Thank you for your concern." She pushed out of his lap and rose, the blanket still around her shoulders. She retrieved her clothes from the table. "May I take the blanket to the locker room with me?" Because she really didn't want to bare herself in front of him. Not any more than she'd already done. Even if he didn't see it—or was purposely ignoring it.

He stood, his slate gray button down still open over his sculpted chest and abs. "Of course." He looked like he wanted to say something else, but he didn't. So Mia left the little lounge. And him.

Threatening tears stung the backs of her eyes. She was just vulnerable after that scene, damnit. That's all this was. Because Mia totally hadn't gone and fallen for the freaking gorgeous orgasm machine of a Dom who'd told her not to do that. Nope. She hadn't been that dumb at all.

Except. Yes. Yep. She totally had.

Head down and rushing in the direction of the locker room, she somehow didn't see the big wall of man she ran into until her nose was smashed against his chest.

"Whoa there, little subbie," he said, amusement in his voice.

"Oh," she said, grateful that he'd steadied her before she'd fallen. "I'm so sorry, Master Quinton." Panic flared, because she really needed to be alone. But interacting with someone else did exactly what she feared and broke down the last of her defenses. Tears filled her eyes.

His expression dropped. "Hey, hey. Don't worry about it, Mia. No harm done," he said, brushing at the corners of her eyes with his hands.

Shaking her head, she clasped a hand over her mouth.

The big Dom folded her into his arms and shepherded her into a more private area. "Tell me what has you so upset."

She shook her head again, embarrassed and still trying to hold herself together, even as she was falling apart. "It's nothing."

"Nothing doesn't make someone cry, Mia," he said. His fingers lifted her chin, forcing her to look at him. His gaze dropped to the blanket she clutched tight around her shoulders, the pile of clothes in her hands. "Did someone hurt you?" His expression darkened.

"No, I promise. It's nothing like that. I appreciate your concern. Truly, I do. But, please, Master Quinton. Please just let me go." She shuddered out a breath.

He looked at her a long minute, and then he kissed her forehead. "Okay, but only if you'll promise to call me if you need anything." He slipped a card into her hand.

She'd talked—and *only* talked—to Master Quinton every night she'd visited Blasphemy. Their conversations were playful and fun and always set her at ease. And he was giving her his contact information and extending his friendship. And yet, Master Kyler…

No. Don't.

"Thank you," she said, grasping the card tightly. And then he let her go. Mia made quick work of changing and getting a cab. The sooner she got away from Blasphemy, the better. No sense wanting something she couldn't have. No sense crying about it, either. Which suddenly made her feel a lot better about not being able to afford the membership. Not being able to see Master Kyler would make it easier not to be able to have him.

At least, that's what Mia hoped.

* * * *

Kyler wasn't going to see Mia again.

She was gone. Not coming back. And he'd let her walk out the door.

He paced the little lounge, the flood of conflicting emotions chaotic in his head. Relief. Guilt. Panic. Gut-deep disappointment. Relief again.

Maybe even a little fear.

Fear that he'd let go of the best chance he might ever have for something more than work and solitude and more work.

He should've stopped her. He should've been honest.

And then, what, genius? Build something good with her only to watch the job tear it all apart year by fucking painful year?

Kyler hated that he'd hurt her, but he'd hate it even worse if it happened after years spent together. It was better this way.

Coward. Yeah, probably. Fuck.

He heaved a deep breath and raked his hands through his hair. If it was better this way, why didn't he feel any better about it?

He stalked out of the lounge, buttoning his shirt as he went. He was on the schedule for the second shift of manning the registration desk in thirty minutes, so at least he'd have something to distract his mind from the clusterfuck of his conversation with Mia.

Back out on the floor, the vibe was vibrant and a little frenetic, busier than usual for a Tuesday night. A seductive bass beat provided a backdrop against which cries of ecstasy and stern commands and free laughter rang out. Normally he loved it. Tonight, he just wanted to escape from it.

At the bar, he braced his arms on the marble top and waited for Griffin to see him. Damn, Kyler was tired. Tired in a way that had nothing to do with sleep.

Griffin gave him a smile when he noticed Kyler at the far end of the circular space. Tall, with close-trimmed black hair and the scruff of an early beard, both sprinkled with a little gray, Griffin was a custom furniture builder who'd done a lot of their carpentry around Blasphemy, including making a few custom pieces of dungeon furniture for the club. "What can I get you?" he asked.

"Whiskey neat," Kyler said.

"You got it," Griffin said, smacking a napkin on the bar top. "How's your night going?" He peered at Kyler as he reached for a glass and the bottle.

Shaking his head, Kyler sighed. "I don't even know, my friend. I don't even know."

"Well I might have an idea," came a deep voice. Quinton leaned into the bar right beside him, his big beefy arm braced against the marble.

"Meaning?" Kyler said, the other man's tone raising his hackles.

Quinton tilted his head and gave him a hard look. "Saw Mia on her way out a few minutes ago."

Griffin put the amber-filled tumbler down in front of Kyler. "Mia's a sweetheart," the bartender said. "Sure hope she joins full time."

"You knew she was a temp?" Kyler asked. How had Griffin known that but he hadn't? Kyler couldn't decide if he was pissed to have let that catch him off guard, or if it was a blessing in disguise. Because now he wouldn't have to keep fighting himself to stay away from her—and losing.

"You didn't?" Griffin's expression was skeptical, then incredulous. "I guess you two weren't doing a whole lotta talking."

Kyler tossed back a swig of the liquor, the heat tearing down his throat a needed distraction from the shit storm in his head.

"I wouldn't be too sure about her joining," Quinton said, his light brown gaze not letting up one bit. "She didn't seem too happy when she left."

What had Quinton seen or heard to make him come to that determination? Guilt slashed through Kyler, and worry, too. Goddamnit.

"Why? What the hell happened?" Griffin demanded, looking between the two men, anger rolling off of him. The guy had a raw spot when it came to a submissive being hurt or injured, one that he'd come by honestly.

"Dunno. Was hoping Master Kyler might shed some insight on that." Quinton raised an eyebrow.

"Kyler?" Griffin asked, nailing him with a dark stare. "What am I missing here? Why was she unhappy?"

Barely restraining a groan, Kyler took another drink. "She can't afford the membership."

Griffin froze, a confused expression on his face. "Can't afford...? But aren't you...?" Kyler didn't need him to finish the thought. When a Dom claimed or collared a sub, he would pick up the membership costs for her. Clearly, the fact that Kyler had dominated Mia's time here had been noticed. And conclusions about what that meant had been drawn.

"Yeah, I kinda thought so, too," Quinton said, that damn eyebrow still arched.

"I don't do relationships. You know this," Kyler said, a big rock parked in his gut. The last thing he wanted to be doing was publicly hashing out the mess he'd made with Mia. He knew perfectly well what he'd done. And his chest felt fucking hollow for having done it. "So you thought wrong."

"That's some bullshit right there, Kyler. But tell yourself whatever you need to sleep at night, I guess." Quinton turned toward Griffin. "Gimme a bottle of water, Griffin?"

"You know what, Quinton? When I need a life coach, I'll fucking hire one." Kyler emptied his glass and slammed it down on the bar.

"Yeah? By the time you do, one of the best things you ever had will be long gone. But suit yourself." Quinton grabbed the water and saluted Griffin with the bottle. "Thanks, G." He walked away.

"Damnit," Kyler said, feeling like an asshole. He was batting zero tonight, wasn't he? He looked up to find Griffin staring at him. "What?"

Griffin scratched at his jaw. "Saw that scene you did with her. The one where you took her while watching my demo. And I've seen you play with other submissives, too. Mia? You and her are like two sides of a coin. Perfectly fucking matched. She's the one you keep, Kyler. She's the one you *collar*. Take it from someone who let the right one get away." He stayed for just another moment, his whole expression darkening, and then he moved down the bar to take someone else's order.

Christ, if he wanted to be hassled, he could take an extra shift riding his desk waiting for Breslin or that IA prick to rain some shit down on him. But that was the problem with having a bunch of Doms for your best friends—none of them could resist telling you what to do. For fuck's sake.

Worse? His heart said they were right, while his gut said his heart was being selfish.

But, damnit, he'd let her go, and she'd been upset.

That cut through him like a jagged knife. He'd failed Mia tonight, as both a man and a Dom.

And maybe that was the best reason of all just to let her go.

Chapter 9

The bar had Mia's favorite mojito, made with real crushed strawberries and sweet, crumbly sugar all around the edge of the glass. She was on her third and feeling fine. Well, as fine as she could feel four days after she realized she'd fallen for a man, a Dom, who didn't want her back.

"Finish that and let's dance," Dani yelled, the volume necessary despite the fact that they were sitting right next to each other. Located down by the Inner Harbor, the bar was one of those awesome joints that went from a cool, relaxed vibe at happy hour to a hip, happening after-hours party at night. Music thumped out a beat that made you want to move, and the lyrics begged to be sung at the top of her lungs. Mia's bestie had come up from Washington for the weekend on a lift-Mia's-spirits campaign after hearing what'd happened with Kyler. Or, rather, *not* happened. Friday night, Dani had allowed them to stay in and devour large quantities of ice cream while watching chick flicks. But tonight, she'd insisted they get dressed up to the nines and go out on the town.

The campaign was working.

Mia was having fun and not thinking about Kyler. Mostly.

Oh, who was she kidding? But she *was* having fun.

Mia took a big swallow, emptying her glass. "Okay, chica. Let's do it."

"Woohoo!" Dani shouted, slipping off the chair and grabbing Mia's hand. They wound their way through the crowd, Dani already dancing as she guided them, until they found a spot in the center of the floor.

Mia let the music wrap around her and move her body, colored lights flashing over her in the darkness, a strobe making the room feel like it was spinning. Her skirt was short but full, and it swished around her thighs, another layer of dizzying sensation. It was awesome. Just what she needed. Freeing and exhilarating.

A man came up behind Dani and leaned his face toward her ear. He was good-looking, with light brown skin and dark, wavy hair that looked like he'd been running his hands through it. Tall, too. Dani nodded to him and gave Mia an *Oh, my God* look. Mia laughed and nodded.

One song morphed into another, the beat grinding, sensual, sex set to music. Dani and her new Latin friend were getting into it, enough that Mia was thinking about using the bathroom as an excuse to give them some alone time. And then someone pressed up close behind her.

Mia glanced over her shoulder into the smiling, interested eyes of a man just a little taller than her. He was attractive enough, though she didn't find him hot, but he had a great smile and could seriously dance. Throwing caution to the wind, she turned toward him and followed his lead. Soon, she found herself grinning and really having fun as his antics, moves, and purposely funny expressions made her throw her head back and laugh.

She knocked into someone as she moved, and then hands settled on her waist. Her gaze whipped to the side, anger at the stranger's presumptuousness on the tip of her tongue.

"You want him, Mia?"

She recognized the voice in her ear before she laid eyes on the speaker.

Master Kyler.

"Do you?" he asked, dark eyes absolutely blazing, his hands gripping her more firmly, his body moving behind hers.

She couldn't pull away despite the chaos erupting in her brain—over the fact that he was here, over the feelings of relief, rightness, and heat rushing through her blood, over the fact that she didn't want to feel anything at all, not if he didn't want her back. "What if I do?" she called over the music.

"You *don't*," he gritted out, tugging her against him to find his cock hard against her lower back. His hands slid upward, inch by slow inch, until they were right beneath her breasts and she ached for him to grab her there. Their bodies moved together, falling into a shared rhythm.

The music changed, the song erupting into an arousing, driving beat that conjured up images of sweaty bodies and twisted sheets. The dance floor went wild. The man with the nice smile and nicer moves offered her a little bow, his gaze flashing to Kyler behind her, before fading away into the press of bodies.

She whirled in Master Kyler's embrace. "You don't get to tell me what I do or don't want, Kyler." Her belly flipped to say his name that way. But he wasn't her Master, was he?

His arms banded around her and his hands moved over her back, holding her close, staking a claim. At least, that's how it felt. But she didn't trust it.

"Maybe I don't," he said, hauling her into him, his thigh pushing between hers, forcing her flowy skirt up to bare more of her legs. The way he moved—the way he moved her—had her brain thinking about all the other times he'd been between her legs, thrusting, grinding, penetrating. Her core clenched at the frustratingly light friction, wanting more, *needing* more. Of him. "But what if I'd like to have a say?"

What the hell did that mean? She pushed at his chest. His closeness made it too hard to think. But he wouldn't let her go. "Mast—" She shook her head, exasperated and overwhelmed. "Kyler, what are you even doing here?"

Blue eyes blazing, his expression was full of that intensity she loved. He leaned his mouth to her ear. "Bachelor party. Was on the way out when I saw you. The others just left. I told them I'd catch up."

She frowned. "Why...why did you do that?"

He got right in her face, their hips grinding together as he guided them, his erection obvious against her. "Because the woman I can't stop thinking about is here."

Mia's heartbeat kicked up inside her chest. *Don't get sucked in.* "Really."

His hand on her back pressed her closer, so close that her breasts crushed against his chest. "Really. She's here and she looks fucking gorgeous and she dances like a goddess intent on bringing me to my knees."

A shiver ran over her skin. At the grit in his voice. At the mental image of him kneeling before her. But Mia didn't know what to say, because she didn't want to read anything into the coincidence of them running into one another. That's all it was. "I'm with a friend."

His face fell into a scowl. "That guy?"

"My girlfriend," she said, nodding over his shoulder.

Kyler followed her gaze to where Dani was still obviously into the same man who'd started dancing with her several songs before. "It looks like she'll be entertained for a little while," he said.

"Well, I don't want to keep you from *your* friends," she said, trying to remain detached despite the fact that he'd made her wet. Damn him.

His hand slid into her long, loose hair, and lightly fisted at the nap of her neck. "Fuck them. I want to be with you."

Oh, God, she was on the verge of climbing him, she really was. And that made her mad. Why did he have to have such power over her body? "Well, what if I don't want to be with you? You were kind of an asshole, you know."

He gave a rueful grin, and that was sexy, too. "Not kind of, Mia. Total. I was a total asshole. And every day since, I've regretted our last conversation. I fucked it up."

Her belly flipped in surprise. Suddenly, a popular dance song came on that had everyone singing and calling out the words. More bodies pressed into the tight space. It was deafening and a little suffocating.

"Would you go upstairs with me? Little easier to talk," Kyler said, pressing his face to hers.

Mia debated. But who was she kidding? He was here, he was interested, and he'd apologized. She should at least hear him out. So she nodded. And tried to ignore the thrill that shot through her body from the way that Kyler held her hand. Finding Dani in the crowd, Mia gestured toward upstairs. Dani winked and grinned obnoxiously. Mia rolled her eyes and mentally prepared for the grilling sure to happen later.

Keeping her body close to his, Kyler guided Mia to the steps leading upstairs. In the front of the bar, a balcony of seating ran all the way around the dance floor, overlooking it. Further back, black curtains hung from the ceiling creating seating areas, some with bigger groups of chairs and couches and some with more intimate spaces comprised of only a love seat and a table. Waiters moved between the groupings.

Kyler took them to the back, where they found an empty love seat. The music wasn't as intrusive here, and the small couch's position created a bit of privacy. He drew her into the space, and Mia had the chance to really drink him in for the first time. He wore a fine black dress shirt that conformed to his muscles, his strong arms, his broad shoulders, his taut chest. She'd never seen him in slacks before, but he looked fucking hot, polished and refined. A look he wore well.

"Sit," he said. "Please." Mia sank into the soft leather, and Kyler sat close beside her, his body turned toward her.

Nervous anticipation jangled through her. "So…about you being an asshole…"

Chuckling, Kyler took her hand and winked. "Yes, about that. I'm sorry because I'd like to see you again."

The room spun around her, despite the fact that she was sitting perfectly still. But then she shook her head. "I can't afford it." She'd received the offer of full membership just yesterday, but between the cost and how she and Master Kyler had left things, she hadn't even given it a second thought.

"I'm not talking about Blasphemy, Mia. Well, not just Blasphemy. I'm talking about me and you." He traced his finger over her thigh, close to her knee.

She shivered, as much from the touch as from the words. "Me and you," she repeated.

"Sounds even better when you say it," he said, leaning in and nuzzling her face. He kissed her temple, her cheek, the corner of her mouth. "I just need you to know, I don't do this, Mia. Any of this. Because I've never before met anyone who made me want to do it. And I'm not even sure I'll be any good at it. But the last few days have been fucking miserable, and I—"

She kissed him. Planted her hands in his hair and kissed him so damn hard. Because she'd heard enough. Enough to know what she wanted.

The growl he unleashed sounded like pure victory, especially when he quickly took over, plundering her mouth with his tongue, hauling her onto his lap so that she straddled him. He tugged her hair, rubbed hard hands over her body, pressed his erection up against her wet panties.

"Oh, God," she rasped around the edge of the kiss.

"Fucking missed you," he said, his hands finally touching her breasts, kneading and squeezing through the thin cotton of the little bronze-colored dress. "Fucking *need* you."

"I need you, too," she rasped, grinding against his erection. Her blood was molten, and a sheen of sweat broke out over her body. She was already so close.

"Don't come," he ordered. His big palm slipped under the flowy pleats of her dress and gripped her ass. Hard. "You do *not* have permission to come."

She whimpered because the command shoved her in that direction, just like he must've known it would. The sexy bastard. "Please, Sir. Please."

He nailed her with a stare, his eyes dark blue fire. "You want to come, Mia?"

A fast nod. "Yes, Sir."

"You want to come, you do it on my cock."

For a second, Mia couldn't breathe, because she wasn't sure she'd ever been so turned on in her whole life. "Here? Now?"

Kyler just looked at her, one eyebrow arched in a challenge, a dare. She gave a single nod.

In a flash of movement, Kyler shifted to retrieve his wallet, and then a condom from within. "Your hands will be on my shoulders or in my hair. You will not make a sound. If someone approaches us, you will sit still and act natural." He smirked at her as he shifted again to unzip his slacks and remove his long, hard length. She watched as he sheathed himself. "Your skirt will cover us. Only you and I will know that your pussy is impaled on my cock. Understood?"

"Yes. God, yes." She couldn't believe they were doing this, but she didn't want to resist. Not for a second. She needed him in her so damn bad it felt more important than her next breath.

"Then put my cock inside of you." He tugged her panties to the side.

Releasing a shaky breath, she took him in hand and lifted so that she could sink down on his length. A moan spilled out from her throat when he bottomed out inside her. She felt deliciously full. It was perfection.

Growling, Kyler pinched her clit. Hard. "No sounds."

She swallowed a threatening shriek as he fixed her skirt. Remembering the rules, she put her hands on his shoulders.

"Ride me, Mia. Slow." His hands fell on her thighs and teased her bare skin.

She started moving. Slow up. Slow down. Every time she was fully seated on top of him, her clit ground against his pants. It only took about a half dozen teasing strokes until her whole body was vibrating with her approaching orgasm.

"Don't fucking come," he said in a low, strained voice.

"Please," she whispered.

"If we weren't in public, I'd stuff your mouth with your panties to keep you quiet," he said, face stern. "Instead…" He tugged the soft fabric down over one breast, and then the cup of her bra. Just enough to bare a nipple. He squeezed her there, twisted, held on until she was panting and trembling from the restraint of holding back. Heat scorched through her, radiating out from the pain in her nipple.

"Good girl," he said. His hand gripped her thigh. Hard. A warning. "Stop."

She froze.

"Can I get you all something to drink?" said a man standing behind Mia. She had a cock inside her, one breast free from her clothing, her nipple being held between Kyler's vise-like fingers.

"Darling?" Kyler asked, smiling. "What would you like?"

Damn him. Damn him and his unaffected voice. But she knew it was an act. She *knew* it was, especially when his cock jerked inside her. "Strawberry mojito," she said.

"I'm sorry, what was that?" the waiter asked.

She peered over her shoulder and tried to smile. "Strawberry mojito, please."

"I'll have a whiskey neat," Kyler said. "Thanks."

She knew the moment they were alone again because Kyler lifted her and slammed her pussy down on his cock in a punishing, glorious thrust. He released her nipple, and the flash of pain was like an electric shock. She could've screamed as a wave of pain sliced through her, but then Kyler was slamming into her again. And again. And again. "Do. Not. Come."

Her fingers were like claws in his shoulders and her whole body shook. The material of his pants, wet now from her juices, added to the torment.

Kyler's gaze was glued to hers as he slowed their bodies back to the earlier, torturous pace and urged her to take over. "That waiter…he knew I was balls deep in you, Mia. He knew and he was so fucking jealous."

She couldn't hold back a whimper. She loved being watched, and loved that Master Kyler understood her need for it and gave it to her like this. It was so deliciously dirty.

"Right now, he's wondering what your pussy feels like. He's fantasizing that it was him making you wet and shaky and hot. He's wishing he could join in." He pulled her down for a kiss that was short and restrained and even sexier for it. Holding her by the neck, he looked deep in her eyes. "In a minute, he's going to return with our drinks. When I tell him 'thank you,' you're going to come. Eyes on me. No sounds. But come. Understand?"

"Yes, Sir," she whispered, the room absolutely spinning around her as she continued to ride him in slow ups and downs that made her crazy but didn't quite get her there. On top of it all, the anticipation of the waiter's return had her heart racing and her skin feeling like an electrical current ran over every part of her.

And then Kyler was gripping her thigh again, stilling her as the waiter placed their drinks on the table behind her. "Here we go," the man said.

Kyler's hand dropped to between her legs, and his fingers secretly found and massaged her clit. "Thank you," he said. Mia gasped at her cue.

"Can I get you anything else?" the waiter asked. But Mia barely heard him because Kyler's fingers tugged on her clit, a hidden, stinging command. The orgasm detonated inside her, stealing her breath as her pussy spasmed so hard that her expression morphed into the shape of a silent scream, her mouth wide, her eyes closed. The waiter had to know. Oh, God, the waiter *had* to know.

"That's all for now," Kyler said. The hard grit in his voice wound her body even tighter.

She barely knew what was happening when Kyler lifted and slammed her down once, twice, three times, dragging her orgasm out even more. He pulled her face down to his and claimed her mouth on a roar that she mostly swallowed. His cock kicked inside her over and over and he shuddered beneath her as his release erupted.

"Fuck," he rasped when his lips parted from hers. "Lift up, baby."

She did, regretting his loss. In a series of quick movements, he removed the condom and tucked himself away. A few wet spots darkened the front of his pants.

He studied her, looking at the mess they'd made. "I fucking hope I smell like you, too." He winked, then nodded at where his hand hid the condom. "Be right back."

She smiled and watched him go. And that man's ass. Geez, that ass was a thing of beauty. For real.

When he returned, Kyler pulled Mia in tight against his side, her knees curled up against his thigh. They drank quietly, both of their bodies still hot from the sex.

"Will you go out to dinner with me?" he asked.

She peered up at him, and the uncertainty in his gaze was totally endearing. Her heart tripped all over itself. Was he really so unsure? Of her, or of himself? "I would love to."

His smile was so damn pleased. "Good. That's good. Would Wednesday night work? I don't think I can wait 'til next weekend to see you again."

Her heart tripped a little harder, falling, falling, falling for him. She kissed him and stroked her fingers through his hair. "Wednesday would be perfect."

Kyler nodded, his expression all pure male satisfaction. "As much as I don't want to, do we need to get you back to your friend?"

"Soon. But, for now, would you just hold me?" she asked, too content to move, too happy with the night's unexpected turn of events to want it to be over.

He kissed her forehead and squeezed her in tighter against the side of his body. "Yeah, baby. Nothing would please me more."

Chapter 10

Kyler Vance was breaking all the rules now. But for nearly the whole week after he'd let Mia walk out of Blasphemy, his gut had demanded he'd played that situation all wrong. Rules be damned.

With everything else that'd gone bad in his life lately—losing Miguel, getting shot, being forced to ride a desk, the investigation—losing Mia was one thing too many, one loss too great.

And if his own instincts weren't pushing him hard enough in the direction of making things right with her, of giving at least something with her a try, Quinton and Griffin wouldn't quit busting his balls every chance they got. And then Griffin had called him out.

"If you're doing so good without Mia, if you've moved on, then do a demonstration scene. Find a new submissive tonight. Right now. You know there are plenty of subs here who'd love to scene with you. Find one and fuck her." Griffin had slapped a Ben Franklin on the bar. Quinton had crossed his arms and given a nod, like he thought it a damn good plan.

And it was. It should've been. But as Kyler had contemplated the bet—as he thought about finding someone, touching her, having her touch him—it had all felt wrong. And that wouldn't have been fair to the submissive.

Kyler had glared at Griffin, much to the other man's amusement. And Kyler had had to admit, if merely *thinking* of being with someone else felt so wrong, actually *being* with someone else was completely off the table. Which meant he'd gotten attached. His feelings had gotten involved. And he wanted more when more was something he never even let himself imagine.

Sonofabitch.

And then he'd run into Mia at that bar on Saturday night, had seen her dancing so seductively with another man, and every fiber of his being had demanded that he claim her once and for fucking all.

Mine.

Damn if that night at the club with her hadn't removed the ten-ton truck that'd been parked on his chest all the week before. And holding her there at the end? That had satisfied parts of himself that he hadn't even realized needed eased.

Now, here he was, knocking on the door of Mia's apartment on the second floor of an old brownstone, dressed in a fucking suit to take her to dinner.

Mia opened the door wearing a smile and a beautiful teal-blue dress that hung all the way down to a pair of tall, peep-toe wedges. She wore her hair loose again, soft and wavy and thick around her shoulders. So damn gorgeous, this woman. "Hi," she said. "I'm ready to go, unless you'd like to come in?"

"Well, I'd at least like to do this." He stepped inside, dug his fingers into the heavy silk of her hair, and kissed her. She hummed at the contact and her body went soft and pliant against him, her breasts pushing into his chest, her spine sagging her weight against him. His hand slid down to grab her ass and gave a little squeeze.

"You don't play fair," she whispered.

Grinning, he pulled back. He loved the arousal in her dark eyes, the humor in her expression. "I'd have thought you knew that by now." He winked.

Her laugh was like the sun breaking through the clouds, warming him and lifting his spirits. And giving him just that much more evidence that he was doing the right thing here, with her.

She rolled her eyes and shook her head.

He grasped her by the jaw. "You know, when you roll your eyes at me, I want to put you over my knee."

A slow grin crept up her face. She rolled her eyes again.

Challenge. Fucking. Accepted.

Pushing the door closed, Kyler grasped Mia by the waist and lowered himself to one knee, laying her over his other knee in the process. She screamed and bucked, but he held her in place with an arm across her lower back. He rucked up her dress, baring miles of lovely legs—and a bare ass, too. She wore no goddamn panties.

"Oh, Mia. Very good," he said. She'd anticipated one of his desires without him having to voice it. He hadn't wanted to put any undue pressure on whatever it was they might be by articulating a list of rules for their time together. He was trying to play it by ear, to see what might be natural between them. Whether that was the right way to go about it, he wasn't sure. But it wasn't like he had a lot of experience at relationships. He ran his palm over her smooth cheeks. "And it's gonna be even better when this ass is nice and pink. Five ought to do it. Count."

His hand came down on the right globe.

"One."

"One, what?" He rubbed her skin, identifying his next target.

"One, Sir." The need in her voice shot to his cock. He spanked the left. "Two, Sir."

Next, his hand landed low and in the center, his fingers making contact with her pussy lips.

"Oh, God. Three. Three, Sir."

By the time she thanked him for the fifth and final spanking, his cock was rock hard. He pushed his fingers between her legs. She was soaking wet.

"Fuck, Mia. I was trying to be a gentleman tonight," he said, arranging her on her hands and knees on the floor and fishing a condom out of his pocket. "But if you want the Dom, I'll give you the fucking Dom."

"Yes, please." Her voice was full of need as she peered over her shoulder at him.

Kneeling behind her, he lined himself up with her wet hole and slammed home. They both cried out. "I want to hear you," he growled. "I want you to be loud." And then he took her hard and fast. Holding onto her shoulders, her throat, a thick chunk of her hair, he rode her until she was moaning and babbling and saying his name over and over like a litany or a spell. Her sounds certainly wrapped themselves around him.

Their orgasms came as hard and fast as their fucking, causing them to sag in a sated pile onto the floor by her front door. Christ, he hadn't even made it past the door. *That's* how bad he had it for her.

When they were done, Kyler carefully lifted her until she knelt right in front of him.

"Be careful, sweetie. Don't issue a challenge you aren't ready to have accepted." He arched a brow at her, loving the high flush on her cheeks, the arousal still heating her dark eyes.

"Yes, Sir. Thank you," she said, a smile playing around her lips.

"Little brat." He kissed her and felt her smile grow under his lips. God, he was in fucking trouble with this woman. He really was. Although he felt lighter than he had in months. Maybe longer. Maybe *ever*.

A short while later, they were walking into a restaurant down near the Inner Harbor. An upscale steak house with an Old World décor, all carved wood, warm leather, and crystal chandeliers. It was the kind of place where people celebrated special occasions or businessmen negotiated big deals. Kyler had just wanted to make a good first impression. Well, a good first-date impression, anyway. Hopefully, taking her on her apartment floor before appetizers counted as a plus in her book.

For fuck's sake.

They ordered champagne and soup and filet mignon and sides to share. Conversation came easily as Mia talked about her work at the gallery and her friend, Dani, who Kyler had briefly met at the bar Saturday night when he'd finally had to stop keeping Mia all to himself. And then her face had really lit up when she'd talked about the kind of mixed-media art she did.

"Mixed media, what does that mean exactly?" Kyler asked.

"It can be anything," Mia said. "Paint, layers of paper, pieces of metal, everyday objects, even technology. Whatever tells the story of the piece." She paused as if debating, then said, "Would you like to see? I have some photographs on my phone…"

"Of course I'd like to see," he said, something deep inside him needing to allay the uncertainty in her voice. "I want to know you, Mia. And your passion for this is crystal clear when you talk about it. I'd love to see what creates that in you."

The pleased expression on her face reached inside his chest. "Yeah? Okay." She retrieved her phone from her little clutch purse and scooted closer to him in the curved booth. One by one, she flipped through a stream of images and described her process and the materials for each one.

"May I?" he said, taking the phone from her and flipping back to a few that really caught his eye. "Mia, your work is fucking amazing. The textures, the layers, the stories, you're really talented."

"Thank you," she said, her smile nearly beaming.

He loved that he'd made her feel that way. Having seen her art, he needed to know more. To know everything. "Does your family live in Baltimore?" he asked.

"Only my dad," she said. "My mom and stepfather live in Philadelphia where I grew up."

"Not too bad for visits, at least," he said. He'd never lived in a different city from his parents. He was a Baltimore boy through and through, from growing up to college to serving on the force.

"No, it's an easy trip," she said with a smile. "And it's been a while since I've lived in the same city as my dad, so I'm really glad for that."

"You two are close?" he asked.

Her expression answered the question before she did. "Yeah. He's kind of a hardass, but he's always been a great father." He loved the passion with which she spoke, the way that her feelings for those she cared about shined from her eyes.

"I'm pretty close to my old man, too. And I think 'hardass' is in the father job description."

She laughed. "That would explain it."

The waiter came and cleared their plates, and they ordered cheesecake to share for dessert. Every part of the meal had been easy and effortless, right down to their shared tastes in food.

"So, I feel like I've been talking too much about myself," she said. "Tell me more about you, Kyler. What do you do for a living?"

His gut dropped. He knew this conversation would come, but he hated the thought that his work might turn her off. And, at any rate, talking about it stirred up his ancient worries that being a cop was a death knell for most relationships. But he'd already decided to let her make those decisions for herself. "I'm a police detective."

Mia froze with her champagne flute halfway to her mouth. And then her expression dropped. She tried to shake away the reaction, but he'd seen it. He'd fucking seen it. "You work for BPD?"

"Yes, Mia. Is that a problem?" His dinner turned into a rock parked in his stomach.

"Uh, no. No, of course not. Just surprised," she said, taking a fast drink of the bubbly.

The waiter brought the cheesecake, a giant piece covered with fresh strawberries and whipped cream. He placed the plate between them and laid two forks on the table. Neither of them reached for one.

"Um." She gave a shaky little laugh and shook her head. "The world is really funny sometimes."

A few men in business suits filed past their table. Kyler did a double take, recognizing a couple of the city councilmen. And, as if his night needed any more awkwardness, Commissioner Breslin was at the back of the group deep in conversation with the council president. Because what everyone wanted was for their boss to witness a date crashing and burning.

Kyler took a drink of his bubbly, the carbonation not doing good things for that rock he felt. "Funny, how?" he managed.

She looked up at the passing men and gasped. "Oh, my God," she said under her breath. And then, when Breslin got right in front of them, she said louder, "Dad, hi. Um, what a surprise."

Commissioner Breslin and Jack Shepard, the council president, stopped at their table. And Mia bore a resemblance to only one of the men. It was all in the eyes. Kyler's boss was Mia's father.

"Mia," Breslin said, looking between his daughter—*his fucking daughter*—and one of the detectives under his command. So much for staying on the commissioner's good side because there was no way the man was going to be happy about this. *No. Way.* Even if her dad was happy about her dating a cop, which Kyler doubted, he surely wouldn't be happy about her dating one under investigation for possible corruption. Jesus Christ.

She slid out of her seat and hugged the man, and it was clear from the expression on Breslin's face that the affection she'd communicated earlier about her father was returned a whole helluva lot.

"Mia, this is City Council President Shepard," her father said as Kyler rose. She shook the other man's hand. "And President Shepard, this is one of my men, Detective Vance." Kyler did the same, and then he offered his hand to his boss.

"Commissioner Breslin. Nice to see you," Kyler said.

"Detective Vance," her father replied, not returning the sentiment. "I'm sorry to interrupt your...date." The last word came out full of surprise and disapproval, hammering the last nail in whatever hope Kyler might've had that this wasn't going to somehow come back and bite him and his career in the ass. Not to mention his relationship with Mia. Sonofabitch.

An awkward silence stretched out.

"You didn't interrupt, Dad," Mia finally said. "I'm always glad to see you. You know that."

Breslin nodded. "Well, I wish I could visit longer, but I'm here on business tonight." He gestured to his colleague. "I'll talk to you soon, babydoll." He squeezed Mia's shoulder. "Vance." A single nod.

"Commissioner." A single nod in reply. Fuck. He was so fucked. How predisposed was the old man going to be to give Kyler the benefit of the doubt now? When he was clearly displeased to see him with his daughter. His *babydoll*.

And God forbid Breslin ever learn any of the more intimate details of their relationship. Because holy fucking shit. Kyler would be lucky to keep all his parts.

"Shall we…um…sit?" Mia asked when it was just the two of them.

Kyler gestured toward the table, and they both sat. But all the easiness between them was gone now. Obliterated.

"So, that's why you thought it was funny that I'm a detective? Because your father's my boss?" he asked, trying to rein in his anger but hearing it in his tone all the same.

"Uh, yeah." She fidgeted with her fork, straightening it next to the dessert plate. "I wasn't certain that you'd know one another, though. Big department and everything."

He emptied his glass, but the sweet champagne didn't come close to being what he needed. "Mmhmm." A long silence passed. And with each passing second, any hope Kyler had allowed to grow that he could have something with Mia melted away.

"Have some cheesecake?" she asked, forcing a smile.

He picked up a fork. Stabbed the creamy cake. Barely tasted it as it went down.

Mia swallowed her bite and dropped her fork back to the table, too. She sighed. "May I please be direct?"

He chuffed out a humorless laugh. "I wish you would."

She frowned, anger sliding into her gaze. "What does that mean?"

He shook his head. He waved at the waiter, silently asking for the bill. Kyler needed to get out of there before his own anger and frustration got the better of him. This wasn't Mia's fault. It was his. His for even trying. "Nothing. Nothing at all."

"Kyler—"

"He's my boss, Mia. My fucking boss. And you're his babydoll." His voice dropped. "Who I tied up and choked and beat and fucked in a public place. Among other things."

The annoyance on her face ratcheted up the turmoil raging inside him. "Why does that matter? Even if we were totally vanilla, we wouldn't be sharing that with him either, would we? I'm almost twenty-eight, Kyler. My father has no say in what I do in my personal life."

"But he has a big say in what happens in my professional one." He nailed her with a stare. Sadness slinked through him. Damn. He'd really wanted this to work out.

She sagged against the back of her seat. "So, what? That's it. Because my dad's a cop, too, we're done?"

He shook his head. "He's not just any cop."

"Right. He's the commissioner. I get it—"

"You don't," he gritted out. The waiter chose that moment to drop off the bill. Kyler tossed a card into the leather folder without looking and urged the man away. He heaved a long, weary breath. "I'm under investigation, Mia. Part of your father's effort to oust corruption in the department. I'm *not* corrupt, and hopefully things will work out the way they should and I'll be cleared. Soon. But I'm already on Breslin's shit list." He shook his head as saying her father's name made him realize. "So your name is Mia Breslin." If he'd have asked, even once, all this could've been avoided. Breslin was too unique of a name to not have cued him in sooner. But he'd been keeping to his rules…and then he'd been foolishly running roughshod right over them. Now, here they were.

"Yep," she said, her shoulders dropping.

The waiter returned with the credit card slip and Kyler scribbled his name in a hard line.

Mia was quiet for a long moment, and he was sure that what he'd revealed about his career must've soured her toward him. Who'd be happy to learn they were dating a potentially dirty cop? Absolutely no one. And certainly not the daughter of a decorated, high-ranking officer. "Look, Kyler, I'm sorry to hear about the investigation," she said. "From everything I've read in the papers, it sounds like it's needed in the department, but I'm sorry that you've gotten swept up in it."

Her words made his chest ache. She believed him? She wasn't suspicious of him? "You're sorry?"

She gave a little shrug. "Of course I'm sorry. My dad was

investigated once years ago and I remember how stressful that was for him."

"So you believe me," he said, the truth of that still not fully computing.

"Yes. Why wouldn't I?" Hurt flashed across her face. "But, I guess, does it even matter that I believe you?"

It mattered. It mattered to him a fucking lot.

"I mean," she continued, "does it matter what I think about that if you've decided that my father being your boss is a deal breaker? For me and you?" Me and you. He'd loved when she'd said those words the other night at the bar. Now, they broke his goddamned heart. Not that his heart was involved. Well, not really. She kept her eyes on his, but he could tell that it was costing her to put herself out there so directly.

Which meant he owed her the same. "No, I guess it doesn't matter. I'm sorry, Mia." And even though on some level, it *didn't* matter, not when her father could ruin Kyler's career, the words still tasted like ash in his mouth. Because they weren't all the way true, either. Mia's belief in him mattered. The affection with which she'd looked at him up until about ten minutes ago mattered. *Mia* mattered. To him.

But you couldn't always have what you wanted, could you? If Kyler could, Miguel would still be alive.

"Well." She dropped her gaze to the white-cloth-covered table. "I see." She grasped her little clutch purse from the seat beside her. "Thank you for dinner, Kyler." In a quick move, she rose and started walking.

He followed, easily catching up with her. "I'll drive you home."

Without looking at him, she shook her head. Her heels clicked against the marble floor. "That won't be necessary, Detective. The valet can call me a cab."

Detective. Fuck. "Mia—"

The rotating doors cut off his effort to talk to her. When he came out onto the street, she was already asking the valet to get her a car. The man stepped out into the road and blew a whistle.

"Mia."

She turned to him, her expression carefully neutral. But her eyes revealed everything. Sadness. Disappointment. Hurt. *He'd* caused that. Every bit of it. "Yes?"

"Miss, your taxi," the valet called.

She looked at Kyler another second, then turned on her heel and made for the car.

Kyler rushed after her, putting his body in the way of the door. He debated for a long moment, but it was already paid for. It was hers, no matter what. He retrieved the little black leather card case from his suit coat. "I...I got this for you. It was going to be a surprise. It's yours. No strings attached, of course." He squeezed her cold fingers.

"Good-bye," she said, not even looking at what he'd handed her.

And then Kyler was watching her drive away from him. And he'd been right. It did fucking hurt more now that he was involved. Which just meant that he'd been right to let her go that night at Blasphemy. To let her go and not follow.

Because the police force always won. And always ruined relationships.

Lesson learned. Hard.

And he wouldn't ever forget it.

Chapter 11

Two weeks later, Mia was standing in the middle of a disaster area. Crates and boxes and packing material littered the shining floor of her gallery, the debris part of the process of unloading some of the newly arrived pieces for the next show that would open in two weeks. Wearing shorts and a T-shirt, she scooped up an armful of paper wrapping and stuffed it in a big trash can.

She was really excited about the upcoming show. The theme was *avant garde* contemporary art, and highlighted work that mixed photography, graphic art, and pop culture. Today's shipment of crates was from one of the five featured artists, and already she could see that she'd been right that these pieces would speak to her own artistic interests.

God, she was lucky to get to do what she did.

A knock on the glass front door drew Mia's gaze. She grinned and rushed across the space, then unlocked the door for her father. "Daddy, what are you doing here?" She stepped back to let him in.

A big brown paper bag in hand, he kissed her cheek. "I was in the neighborhood."

She snorted. "Not likely, but I'm glad you came anyway. Though it's kind of a mess in here."

"Creative genius at work." He gave her a wink.

"Ha, exactly." She waved him toward the back. "We can sit in my office. Is that Thai I smell?"

"Yep," he said.

"Oh, man. You're the best." She shifted some things on her desk to make room. "Pull that chair up."

He did as she asked and unpacked container after container. "Of course I'm the best. You don't need lunch to prove that."

Mia chuckled and grabbed bottles of water from the staff kitchen right next door. "No, I don't," she said, returning. "But how the heck did you get away in the middle of the day?" They spooned food onto paper plates.

"I'm the boss. If I say I want to play hooky with my daughter, there's no one to tell me no." He grinned, and she smiled back. But his word choice sucked her back to that terrible night with Kyler, the night everything fell apart. Who would've thought that even another cop would get freaked out by the fact that her father was a cop? Granted, the fact that her father was Kyler's boss was a complicating factor, but she'd never known her dad to do anything but support the things that made her happy. And she didn't know why that would change now.

And Kyler? He had made her happy. Really happy. For a while.

God, why did she still miss him so much? Why did not being able to see him hurt so bad? But she did miss him, and it did hurt. Even more because he hadn't been willing to even talk about finding a way to make it work. Had she meant so little?

All of which was why she'd returned Kyler's gift—a year's full membership to Blasphemy. She wouldn't have been able to tolerate seeing him there with another submissive, and therefore she wasn't going to use it, and she knew what it must've cost him. So she'd dropped it into the mail to the club, one of the two possible addresses she had. The other was police headquarters, and no way was she mailing her Blasphemy membership card to him there.

But even with the card out of sight, her brain wouldn't let go of the fact that he'd purchased it for her in the first place. Which was something a Dom did for his submissive, one he claimed, one he collared. Had he been planning…?

No. She had to stop torturing herself by wondering about things she could never know.

"What has you upset, babydoll?" her father asked.

Mia realized she'd been staring at her plate, moving the noodles around with the plastic fork. "Oh. Sorry. Just a lot on my mind. The new exhibit and everything." She waved her utensil dismissively.

Her dad nailed her with a stare, his eyes dark and full of concern. "So, there's this thing I do at my job sometimes called interrogation. And to do it right, I have to be able to tell the difference between the truth and a lie…" He arched a brow.

"Yeah, yeah, yeah," she said, having heard this particular bit of sarcasm before. She took a big bite of the spicy, delicious noodles.

"So?"

"It's nothing I want to talk about, then. How's that?" She shrugged. "I'm fine, though."

"It's Detective Vance." He poured more of the drunken noodles onto his plate and speared an additional potsticker with his fork.

"Dad." Just hearing Kyler's name made her belly hurt and chased her appetite away.

"Mia, a cop isn't who I'd want for you—"

"*Daaad.*" She really didn't want to talk about this.

He reached across her desk and took her hand. "Just listen for a minute. A cop isn't who I'd want for you, because being in a relationship with one is hard. And it's not something most people understand enough to fully realize just how demanding it can be. Of all people, you probably do. But that makes me not want it for you even more."

"Well, you don't have to worry because I'm not seeing Kyler." She met his gaze, then quickly looked away.

"I know," he said. "At least, I guessed. Not from you, but from him."

What did that mean? Mia was dying of curiosity, but she wasn't going to ask. Anyway, did it matter? It'd been two weeks and she hadn't heard from Kyler once. He had her cell phone number and her address. He hadn't used either. "So, why are we talking about him then?"

"Because it's not just that he's a cop that gives me pause." He took another bite.

"He told me about the investigation, if that's what you're going to say," she said.

His expression shifted from surprised to approving. "I'm glad he did, but that's not what I was going to say. I was going to say that I'd be hard-pressed to meet a man I thought was worthy of you, babydoll. Any man." He gave a rueful smile. "Though I know that choice is yours, not mine. I know I wasn't the friendliest the night I ran into the two of you. So if I had anything to do with the fact that you're not seeing each other, I'm sorry. I don't want to mess up with you just when we've finally managed to land in the same city after all this time."

The sentiment made tears prick at the backs of her eyes. "You didn't mess up."

"Good. But you're still unhappy." He frowned.

She smiled, but it quickly faded from her face. "It happens." What else could she say?

They finished eating and her dad left, but now he had her thinking about Kyler, where earlier in the day she'd been distracted by the excitement of the newly arrived pieces for the show. She worked through the afternoon and into the early evening hoping to find her excitement again, but it felt like it was just out of reach.

Part of her wished she'd kept her Blasphemy membership. It would be painful to see Kyler, but maybe if she did, maybe she could tell him...

What?

Hey, Kyler. Guess what? My dad said he doesn't disapprove of us. Want to get back together now?

Ugh. Lame.

Because what a twenty-seven-year-old woman really wanted to do was have to convince a man to be with her. Using her father's permission as a selling point.

The ridiculousness of that made Mia laugh out loud, the sound echoing in the large space of the gallery.

Bone tired, she cleaned up the last of the trash, turned out the lights, and locked up.

Later, when she was in her bedroom and comfortable in her pajamas, Mia spied Master Quinton's card on her dresser. Her heart gave a little pang for him, too. Not because she was interested in him sexually or romantically, but because she felt like he could've been a friend. And it felt like one more loss.

Dropping onto the edge of her bed, Mia debated. And then she shot off a quick text message. *Hi, Master Quinton. It's Mia Breslin. We met at Blasphemy last month. Just wanted to thank you again for your kindness that night.*

She read it over once, twice, feeling kinda stupid. But there was a question she'd been thinking about, and he might be able to answer it. Or refer her to someone who could. On a yawn, she reached to plug her cell into the charger on her nightstand when it buzzed.

He'd written back already? She smiled. Yes, he had.

You've been thinking about my superpowers, haven't you? Admit it. Q

Laughing, Mia nodded. *How could I not? Who can resist a great mystery?* She stared at the phone, hoping he'd write back again.

He did. *When are you coming back in?*

The smile dropped off her face. What should she say? *I don't have a membership.* She stared for another minute, then added. *I was actually hoping you might be able to recommend another club in Baltimore. I love Blasphemy but it's outside my range.*

Her phone rang immediately. Master Quinton's number.

Mia's heart thundered in her chest as she answered. "Hello?"

"Mia, I'm not your Dom," he said by way of greeting, "but I'm about to give you an order. You ready?"

"Um. Maybe?"

His deep chuckle came down the line. "Get your ass over here right now."

"What? I'm in pajamas."

"This is Blasphemy. Clothing is entirely optional. Problem solved. What else you got?" he asked, humor plain in his tone.

"Master Quinton, maybe you didn't get my last text. I can't come back to Blasphemy—"

"I got it," he said. "You can come back. You have a membership."

"I returned it," she said, shaking her head.

"Uh huh. Which is why your card is waiting for you at registration. Memberships are nonrefundable, Mia. You have one. Please use it. This is the only place where I can guarantee your safety, especially given some of your interests."

Meaning the breath play, no doubt. She sighed, confusion and competing reactions roaring through her.

"Are you on your way yet?" he asked.

She chuckled, a little exasperated. "Anyone ever tell you you're bossy?"

He barked out a laugh. "All the fucking time. See you in less than thirty." He hung up.

"Wait—" She groaned and flopped back on the bed. Now what was she going to do?

Her phone buzzed. *Better get moving, little subbie.*

Oh, my God. Why were Doms such pains in the asses? She chuckled, the pun tripping her tired, stupid-humor buttons. But she got out of bed, freshened up, brushed her hair into a ponytail, and put on an easy but sexy black cotton sheath dress with a big, deep cut-out in the back. "Good enough," she said to her reflection.

Mia arrived at Blasphemy with three minutes to spare. At the registration desk, she picked up her card and asked after Master Quinton. She found him tending bar.

"There she is," he said, his handsome face breaking into a big smile. He poured a glass of champagne before she'd even settled into the chair. "On the house."

"Aw, you're too good to me, Master Quinton." Seeing him again was bittersweet because she wasn't at all sure coming here was a good idea.

"No such thing," he said, winking. "Get your card?"

She smirked. "Yeah. Still not sure, though."

He shook his head. "Nothing to be sure about. It's yours whether you use it or not. Might as well use it." He gave her a pointed look.

She nodded and sipped at her champagne.

Mia hadn't come to play. She wasn't in the mood. But she enjoyed the music and the champagne and the company of talking to Master Quinton in between his other customers. But it was late, and she had another long day of work in front of her tomorrow. She waved for her friend, because that was definitely how he felt to her, and Master Quinton made his way back to her. "I'm going to head out. Thanks for ordering my ass here tonight. It was good to see you."

He gave her a crooked smile. "Good to see you, too. Don't wait too long 'til it happens again."

"Yes, Sir."

"Good girl." He winked.

On her way back to the front of the club, Mia stopped at the restroom. When she came out again, she froze in her tracks. Because Kyler was standing at the far end of the hallway. Looking right at her.

Her belly went for a loop-the-loop. There was no way to avoid him. And, if she was seriously going to consider taking Master Quinton's advice, she was going to have to face him sooner or later. Might as well be now.

"Master Kyler," she said, giving him a cool nod. Her body tightened in his presence, muscle memory of all the incredible things they'd shared.

"Mia, I'm glad to see you've come." Thick arms crossed, back against the wall, he was even sexier than she remembered. Damn him.

"Your gift was far too generous, but I understand it can't be returned."

"That's right. So please use it." He met her gaze, and she couldn't read anything in his eyes. Not anything at all.

But what did his words mean? Use it so they could play together? Or use it and play with someone else? Anyone else? What did she have to lose by asking? Because part of her needed to know what he'd say. "Use it to be with you? Or..."

He flinched. She would've sworn he did. He shook his head. "I don't think that's a good idea. But there are...plenty of other..." He shifted feet and raked a hand through his hair. "Others who will be better. For you."

A sickening tingling spread outward from her belly. He really didn't want her. And he was encouraging her to play with or find someone else. "Sure, sure." She crossed her arms, anger and hurt flooding through her anew. "So, what would you recommend? Are Friday and Saturday the best nights to meet someone? Is there another Blasphemy Master you think I should meet? I mean, Master Quinton is pretty awesome. What do you think of him for me? I'd love your advice," she said, screwing with him.

His eyes narrowed on her, heat sparking in the dark depths. "Uh, well..." Discomfort rolled off of him, and not a little agitation, too.

She sighed. "Bye, Kyler. See you on Friday night, if you're around." Because his idiocy was pressing her buttons, making her resolved not to let him run her off from this place she loved and this lifestyle she needed.

Yeah, she'd be back. She'd be back and ready to move on. From him.

Chapter 12

Captain Burkett caught Kyler in the hall. "Your investigation has been concluded. Word just came down to me. I don't know anything else yet, but we've got a four o'clock meeting with Breslin and Foster. Upstairs in the commissioner's office. Don't be late."

"I won't. Do you have any sense of the findings?" Kyler asked, his gut twisting in anticipation and a little fear, too. Because everything he cared about was on the line. Being a detective, protecting and serving, carrying on the family legacy.

Not everything, a little voice interjected. *Not Mia.*

But Kyler shoved that whole line of thought away. That wasn't going to happen. No matter how hard it was going to be to watch her find someone else at Blasphemy, she wasn't his. Even if he thought her father might come around to accepting them and even if they could beat the odds and survive despite the demands of his job, both of which were seriously fucking debatable, Kyler had now pushed her away on multiple occasions. Fuck, he'd told her to find someone else—a fact that made him want to puke every time he remembered the stricken look on her face. His second chance with her had come and gone several times over now. He'd had a shot—a long shot—at something great, but even if he could see a way around all the obstacles, he'd fucked it up. And he couldn't imagine what would make her take him seriously again.

Assuming he wanted to ask that of her.

Which he didn't.

Except he kinda did.

Fuck.

This was why he didn't do relationships.

The day crawled until his meeting, and Kyler was a fidgeting, caffeine-overloaded mess by the time he and Burkett were being called into Breslin's office.

The four men settled around the meeting table at the far end of the commissioner's office.

Foster started speaking, a long preamble about the investigation's purpose and process. Kyler was on the verge of losing his fucking mind. "Can you please cut to the chase?"

The IA guy looked bored. "You've been cleared, Detective. As soon as you can meet your target-shooting qualifications, you can return to duty. There won't be any permanent mark on your personnel file."

Elation roared through Kyler's blood. "I'm cleared? It's really over?" He glanced from one man to the other and found his captain smiling and nodding. And the news was even better because two days ago, for the first time, he'd come within points of passing those quals. He was going to beat the consequences of this injury. His arm and shoulder were getting stronger with each workout, each physical therapy session, each new round of shooting practice. For the first time, he breathed a sigh of relief because he actually believed he was going to get his life back now. He hadn't really believed it until this moment.

"Congratulations, Detective Vance," Burkett said, rising. He offered his hand, and they shook.

"Thank you, Captain." Kyler gave Foster a nod and then looked at Commissioner Breslin. Kyler had seen him around headquarters, of course, but this meeting was the first time since the uncomfortable conversation at that restaurant that they'd spoken.

Breslin rose and offered his hand. "I'm glad it worked out, Detective."

"Thank you, sir."

"You're dismissed," Breslin said.

Burkett clapped Kyler on the back as they turned from the table. They were almost out the door when Breslin spoke again.

"Detective, one more thing?"

Kyler retraced his steps into the big office. "Sir?"

"Detective Foster, would you give us the room, please?"

The IA investigator blinked up. "Oh, of course." He slipped out of the office, and Burkett left, too. The door closed behind them.

Here it came. The warning away from his daughter. Kyler had been expecting it for weeks, so he wasn't surprised it was coming. Though delivering it on the heels of his good news seemed kinda harsh. For fuck's sake.

But at least the man hadn't let knowledge of Kyler dating his daughter impact the investigation. He had to respect that much.

Breslin finally sighed. "What you do on your personal time is your business, Detective."

Kyler waited. And waited. Okay. What the hell was that supposed to mean? "Yes, sir."

"It's none of my business."

The fuck? What was happening right now? "I appreciate that," Kyler managed.

"Aw, for Christ's sake," Breslin said. "Were you this dense with Mia, too?"

The commissioner could've smacked him over the head with a frying pan and Kyler would've been less surprised. "Uh, probably."

Breslin smiled, and then the smile grew into a chuckle. "Yeah. Well, then stop that bullshit now and get your head out of your ass."

Was he...giving Kyler permission to date his daughter? Or his blessing? Or, at the very least, not threatening to cut off Kyler's dick? Because that's what it seemed like. "Uh, roger that, sir."

"We clear here?" Breslin gave him a pointed look.

Kyler inhaled to reply in the affirmative, but other words came tumbling out. "You seriously have no reservations about your daughter dating a cop?"

Breslin dropped into the chair behind his desk and gave him a droll stare. "Only about a million."

"Then why—"

"I have my reasons. The rest is between the two of you." The man clasped his hands over his stomach, his eyes observant and open.

Kyler grasped the back of one of the leather chairs. His brow furrowed as he debated.

"What's on your mind, Kyler?"

He met Breslin's dark eyes, so like Mia's. And in that moment, the two men in that room weren't boss and employee, they were just two men who cared about the same woman. "My parents divorced. My grandparents. I was trying to stay away. Because I didn't want to do that to Mia."

The older man tilted his head, giving him an appraising look. "Lots of jobs are hard on relationships. And not a single relationship offers any guarantees. You get out of a relationship what you put in. And Mia's a hundred-and-ten-percent kinda woman. So I guess I have to ask, what kind of man are you?" He arched a brow.

Well, fuckity fuck. When he put it like that…

When he put it like that Kyler suddenly saw the whole pile of his rationalizations and justifications melt away like a sand castle made without any water, soft and unable to hold shape.

Could it really be that easy? Not the relationship itself, but the leap of faith that they could *make* it work. If they wanted it and fought for it hard enough.

And, oh shit, just two nights ago he'd told her to find someone else to play with. And she'd said she'd see him this weekend. Which meant, she'd be at Blasphemy tonight.

"We clear *now*?" Breslin asked.

"Crystal, sir." Kyler's heart thundered in his chest, urgency rushing through him.

"Glad to hear it, Detective. Dismissed."

Kyler came to attention, then turned and left before Breslin changed his mind.

Back at his desk, the room wouldn't stop spinning. Because what the commissioner said could change everything. If Kyler let it.

Question was, did he really want to open himself up that way again?

The answer pounded through him with every beat of his pulse. *Yes. Yes. Yes.*

Because Mia…Mia was worth the risk. Mia was worth everything.

Don't be a goddamned coward, Vance.

Fuck. *Fuck.*

He dropped his head into his hand and scrubbed at his face. Fact, he wanted her. Fact, not too long ago, she'd wanted him. Fact, the things he thought stood in their way no longer did—or maybe they *never* had, and he'd had his head up his ass just like Breslin said. Fact, Mia was going to be looking for another play partner. Fact, he didn't want her to find one.

Which meant he had to make amends. And he had to do it in a big way. Because unlike that first time, a simple apology wasn't going to cut it this time. He knew that into his very soul.

Looking at his watch, Kyler found that he had two hours until Blasphemy opened its doors, maybe four until things really got hopping. Opening an e-mail, he read over the schedule to see who was on tonight. Master Griffin was on the registration desk. Perfect. He shot off a text.

Can you please let me know if Mia Breslin shows up tonight?

No doubt the other man was going to have a field day with this, but it would be worth it. Worth it to have a chance with her.

Griffin's reply came back quickly. *About fucking time.*

Kyler shook his head and put away his phone. He checked out a few things online, and then he grabbed his jacket and headed out.

Because he had a woman to win back tonight. He just hoped he wasn't too late.

* * * *

Blasphemy was crowded and pulsing with life, the sounds of sex and submission in the air. Mia had gone out and purchased a new leather mini-dress with spaghetti straps, a zipper that ran from the low neckline to the short skirt's hem, and a plunging back. She'd needed the confidence boost of something new and sexy and fun.

Making her rounds to watch the different public scenes, she chatted with a few people, but no one who truly captured her attention. She stopped at a ménage scene with a woman bent over and tied down to a fuck bench. One Dom hammered into her from behind, while another mercilessly fucked her mouth.

Taking it all in, Mia's pulse raced and her core grew wet. What would that be like? She'd never had multiple partners at once before, and it was something that definitely intrigued her. And clearly turned her on.

And it would be different from being with Kyler, a little voice whispered.

"How are you tonight?" came a deep voice.

Mia turned to the Dom, tall and tan, with shoulder-length blond hair. Beside him stood another man, a little shorter, but seriously built, and with a close buzz cut of his dark hair. The blond especially radiated the kind of hallmark authority of a true Dom. Mia's body hummed, recognizing it instantly.

"I'm good, thank you," she said with a smile.

"I'm Jonathan," the blond man said. "And this is Cruz."

Mia shook their hands and gave them her name. They both wore the cuffs identifying Blasphemy's Master Dominants.

"We've been watching for a potential play partner," Cruz said, stepping closer. "You caught our eye. We couldn't help but notice how interested you were in the scene."

"Yes, I was," she said, her heart racing in anticipation.

"Have you ever done a threesome, Mia?" Jonathan asked.

"No, Sir." She glanced from one man to the other, finding both of them attractive. Their faces, their bodies, their personas. Excitement made her belly flip-flop. Any reservations her mind—or her heart—tried to raise she shoved right aside. What choice did she have?

"Would you like to talk about doing a scene with the two of us?" the blond man asked.

A shiver raced over her skin. Was she really doing this? "Yes, Sir, I would."

Jonathan slipped his hand into hers. "Let's find a place to sit," he said. Cruz stepped in close to her other side. Already, they made her feel surrounded and a little overwhelmed. They led her to a small out-of-the-way grouping of couches on the balcony overlooking the nave. She could see everything from up there. Everyone. She looked away, not wanting to see Master Kyler. Not wanting to think of him at all. It hurt too much.

Jonathan guided her to the middle of a love seat, and he and Cruz sat on either side of her. Their heat warmed her and made her hot, inside and out.

"Since this would be your first time, why don't we talk about what you'd most like to experience, and what you wouldn't want to, too." Jonathan brought their clasped hands to his mouth and kissed her knuckles.

It was sweet and sexy. *Kyler*.

Argh! Let it go, Mia. Let *him* go.

She nodded. "I would definitely be open to sex and oral. I've never done anal, and I've never done double penetration."

"Including vaginal double penetration?" Jonathan asked, his brown eyes paying full attention to her.

Her stomach flipped at the thought. It was scary and exciting at the same time. "No, I haven't."

Cruz scooted forward beside her and leaned in. "Are you willing to try those? Or are they hard limits for you?"

Maybe not with the right person, Sir.

The memory came back to her in a flash of sound.

Has anyone ever had your ass, Mia?

"Soft limit on toys for either, and a hard limit for more. At least for my first time," she managed, trying so hard to stay fully present in this moment, with these men.

Cruz nodded. "Toys can be fun." He winked.

She smiled. But she was screaming inside. Because she liked these guys. She was attracted to them. They wanted something with her that she wanted to try. And yet a part of her was dying to even consider doing it. Because that part of her couldn't stop wanting something she couldn't have.

Someone she couldn't have.

Jonathan led them through a conversation about the ribbons on her cuffs, seeking out more knowledge of her interests and limits. "The breath play is a hard limit for us, Mia. We just don't believe that it's safe for the submissive. Will that be a problem for you?"

"No, Sir," she said, her stomach dropping a little. "I understand."

"Good." He smiled. And it was a nice smile. A sexy one. But not Kyler's.

"Excuse me, gentlemen. Jonathan. Cruz. I apologize for interrupting."

Oh, no. That voice. Mia's gaze cut up to find Master Kyler standing in front of them. Heat roared into her face, but she wasn't doing anything wrong, damnit. Certainly nothing to feel embarrassed about.

Jonathan rose. "Of course, Master Kyler. May we help you?"

"Well, actually, it's Mia I need." His gaze bore into hers.

He needed...her?

Jonathan frowned, and now Cruz stood too.

"We're about to start a scene, Master Kyler," Cruz said.

"I understand, and I am sorry. Perhaps we could leave it to her to decide? Mia?"

Three sets of eyes turned to her. She wanted to kill Master Kyler. She really did. Why was he doing this to her when he was the one who'd told her to find someone else? Well, she had. She'd found two someones. Look at her being an overachiever.

"What do you need, Master Kyler?" she asked, not moving from her seat.

"In private, please?" he said. His blue gaze was imploring and intense. But she'd been on this ride. Twice. And she didn't think she could stand getting thrown off of it a third time.

She stared at him, and even after everything, he still appealed to her more than any other man she'd ever met. Now that she knew he was a cop, maybe that was part of it. The swagger, the drive to serve, the willingness to protect others at great personal risk to himself. It made him even more attractive to her, and that made her yearn.

She shook her head, trying so hard to be strong. "I'm not sure that's a good idea."

His jaw ticked. "Mia, I really need to talk to you."

"We did talk," she said. "You told me to find someone else. I have. These men are interested in me. These men *want* me."

"Fucking hell, Mia. *So do I.*" He raked his hands through his hair, and when he spoke again, his voice was softer but every bit as urgent. "I want you so bad I can hardly think straight. I can't concentrate. I can't sleep. I can't eat. For weeks."

"Christ," Cruz said. "We didn't realize you were involved." He looked from her to Kyler and back again.

"We're not," Mia said, his words shocking her and pulling her heart in a million different directions.

"We were," Kyler said at the same time.

Jonathan and Cruz exchanged a glance, and then Jonathan crouched beside her and took her hand. "If you want, come find us when you're done. I hope it works out the way you want."

"I'm sorry," she said. "I really didn't mean for this to happen."

"I know. If we could all keep the emotions out of the sex, things would be a lot less complicated, eh?" He winked.

The two Doms left, but not before throwing less-than-pleased looks at Kyler. He didn't even seem to notice.

She crossed her arms and hugged herself. "They're gone. Satisfied?"

Kyler came right up to her. And dropped to his knees. "Satisfied? That I hurt you? That I failed you? That I made you feel unwanted? That I let fear get the best of me? No, Mia. I could never be satisfied with any of that. I hate it. And I know you've already given me a second chance. I probably don't deserve another. In fact, I'm sure I don't. But on the slim fucking possibility that you ache for me the way I ache for you, I'm here asking for one anyway."

Seeing him on his knees for her reached right into her chest and tugged. Hard. "I don't understand. What's changed? My father is still your boss. I'm still his *babydoll* who you feel uncomfortable tying up and choking and beating and fucking. Right? Isn't that what you said? Or what? Spell it out for me, Kyler. Because you're making my head spin."

He started unbuttoning the navy blue shirt he wore, his eyes locked on hers. "I realized I was letting fear hold me back, Mia. My parents' marriage didn't survive my father being a cop. Neither did my grandparents'. And these past months, I've been terrified that I was going to lose my job. At first, it wasn't because of the investigation. I got shot. That's what all the scars on my shoulder are from, and it caused nerve damage in the joint that reduced my long-distance shooting accuracy. I've been pushing myself through physical therapy, and it's getting better, but if I can't beat this, I'm done. And that was *before* the investigation hit." He shrugged off the shirt, and she swallowed hard. His body was so gorgeous, masculine and rugged and raw. Unconsciously, she leaned forward, as if they were magnets that couldn't help but attract.

Her gaze settled on the scars on his shoulder. Getting shot is what led to his needing surgery? Fear shivered through her, a fear she'd carried her whole life because of what her father did. Mia hated to hear about Kyler getting shot, being injured, suffering. She knew enough to know that these were things she'd always have to worry about, being with him. But would she really run from perfection just because later there might be pain?

He tossed his shirt aside and reached to remove a bandage from his ribs.

"Oh, God. Are you hurt?" She slid off the couch, coming down to her knees in front of him.

"No. Not hurt at all." Removing the bandage was a slow process, and she flinched every time he sucked in a breath. And then it was off.

Mia gasped.

"Kyler. That's…that's like my piece." One of the ones she'd showed him on her phone that night. Her mouth dropped open as she stared at a large tattoo that ran down the side of his ribs under his left arm. The original painting included a mix of oil paints, clock and watch parts, tiny glass beads, photographs of eyes, and metal numbers she'd handmade from scraps. Called "Time," the work was one of her favorites, with the words "The Time is Now" set amidst a chaotic field of time pieces and watching eyes. What was on his ribs wasn't identical, but the inspiration was clear. Her gaze ran over the words, the different sized clocks, some of them in pieces, the numbers. The tattoo artist had done the original work's background colors—varying shades of reds, rusts, dark browns, and creams—in a soft watercolor style that worked perfectly on skin.

"I tried to remember it. To include as many of the details as I could. I haven't been able to stop thinking about it since you showed it to me at dinner that night. I haven't been able to escape the feeling that I was *supposed* to see your art, Mia." He met her gaze, and there was an uncertainty there, like he thought she might be mad.

But she'd never been more honored in her life. He'd put her art on his skin. Permanently. And talked about how it moved him, changed him. What artist didn't want her work to impact someone that way?

"The tattoo artist did an amazing job," she whispered, absolutely awed.

"Jeremy. He loved doing this. And would love to meet you and see your work sometime. If you wanted."

Mia reached to touch Kyler, to trace her fingers over her work on his body, but then she noticed the puffy red around the edges of the ink. She drew back.

"Touch me," he said, grasping her hand and pressing it to the new tattoo.

"I don't want to hurt you," she said.

"You couldn't, Mia. Not by touching me. You make me feel alive. With every touch. Every smile. Every laugh." His voice was full of gravel and emotion.

"Kyler..." Her words trailed off. She could hardly tell a man who'd just inked a part of her into his very skin that he didn't know what he wanted. Because talk about a commitment. "I don't know what to say."

He took both of her hands in his. "I don't just want you for a scene, Mia. And I don't just want you in here, at Blasphemy. I want you in my bed, at my house, in my life. Come home with me. Tonight. Now."

Mia's heart thundered and her pulse beat against her skin. But now she was the one who fear was getting the better of. Because she wanted this—wanted him—so badly. "I'm scared you're going to change your mind."

He came closer, so close that their faces touched. "I won't. My heart won't let me. Because for the first time in my life, I've fallen in love. I've fallen in love, Mia, with you."

Chapter 13

"You...you love me?" Mia said, her eyes glassy. "I...I..." She shook her head. "I'd like to go home with you, Kyler. Can we please get out of here?"

Kyler had them off the floor in an instant. He took tight hold of her hand and guided her back through the club, not stopping for anything. Because it hadn't escaped his notice that she hadn't returned his words—and maybe she wouldn't, or couldn't, just yet. That was fair given everything he'd put her through. But it made him desperate to continue their conversation. It made him desperate to see her in his space. He needed Mia all to himself. Now.

The short car ride felt like a cross-country trip, but finally he was parking at the curb just down the street from his row house. He rounded the front of his Explorer and opened her door, helped her down, took her hand again. He couldn't stop touching her.

Up at the front door, they paused while he inserted the key. He gently grasped her chin and looked at her. "Never brought anyone here before."

Her eyes went wide. "No one?"

"You're the first. In all kinds of ways."

Mia's expression went so, so soft. It gave him hope. Hope that if she wasn't where he was now, she might be able to get there.

Kyler pushed open the door and gestured for her to go first. The living room was small and well lived in, with casual couches, a big TV, and a dog bed on which his old man of a dog laid. Brewster lifted his head and gave him his trademark expression that looked like he was smiling. "That's Brewster. He's nearly deaf." With some effort, the Rottweiler got off the bed and came over to them, a lot of the black on his face heavily speckled with gray.

Mia crouched and held out her hand. "Well, aren't you a handsome man?"

Brewster wasn't usually a licker, but he gave her fingers a few swipes of his tongue. She grinned and stroked his head and ears.

"Oh, don't get sucked in to petting his ears. Once you start, he won't let you stop," Kyler said.

As if on cue, the Rottie sat up tight against her legs and leaned into her so hard that he knocked her over. She laughed out loud as she tumbled into a sitting position on her butt, the big beast half in her lap.

"I'm sorry," Kyler said, rushing to make Brewster get up. "Go on, buddy. You're not helping me out here."

Mia smirked. "He's fine. I don't mind. I grew up with dogs." She grasped the dog's big head in her hands and kissed his face. "I'll pet you more later, okay?"

Brewster looked up at him with a face that said, *Can we keep her? I'm working on it, buddy. I'm working on it.*

"Would you like the nickel tour?" he asked, helping her up.

"Definitely," she said. The place was only fifteen hundred square feet, with two bedrooms and a finished basement, but he showed her all of it, ending in his bedroom. "You have a nice place, Kyler. Thank you for sharing it with me."

"Thank you for coming home with me," he said, walking up to her and putting his hands on her hips. "I don't expect anything from you tonight, Mia. I just want to be with you."

She looked at him a long moment, and then she rested her hands on his chest and met his gaze. "I…Kyler—" She sighed, like she couldn't find the words.

"You can say anything to me. What is it?" He stroked one hand through her hair, so pretty and soft around her face, her shoulder.

"Say it again," she said.

He frowned. "You can say anything to me?"

"No. What you said at the club. Say it again." Her dark eyes burned.

Hope lit in his gut, then a little brighter. Could she mean…? "I've fallen in love with you?"

She nodded. "Yes, that."

Elation roared through him, a wave that wanted to lift him up and up and up. Such an unusual feeling. For him. He cupped her face in his hands. "I've fallen in love with you, Mia. I'm in love with you. And I want you every way I can have you. For as long as you'll have me."

"Oh, Kyler. I…I love you, too."

The words warmed parts of him he thought would always be ice cold. "Aw, Christ, thank you." He wrapped her in a tight embrace, and when her arms came around his back, it nearly took him to his knees. He pulled away and cupped her face again, and then he sealed their words with a searing hot kiss. "Thank you," he whispered around the edge of their kiss. "Thank you for not giving up on me."

"Thank you for not giving up on yourself," she said.

"Mia, I...I have something... Shit. I'm moving too fast, I know it." He scrubbed a hand over his face. He'd never done this before, but he suddenly wanted it as much as he wanted his next breath. Maybe more.

She gave him an uncertain smile. "You can say anything to me, too, you know."

"Yeah?" he said, really wanting to give her the gift he'd bought. Because he knew it would be perfect. On her. When she was ready.

She nodded. "Show me."

His heart a freight train in his chest, Kyler opened the drawer on his nightstand and drew out a large square velvet jewelry box. "I'd love for you to wear this when you're ready, but I don't want to pressure you. I know we have a lot to figure out."

With shaking hands, she took the box and eased it open. "Oh, my God. It's so gorgeous." She traced gentle fingertips over the wide, sleek Herringbone chain. In the center, the chain connected to a heart lock pendant with a large diamond in the middle next to the tiny keyhole. The key hung on a little hook in the middle of the box. She peered up at him. Need shined so brightly from her face.

"Would you be willing to wear my collar someday, Mia?" he asked, an answering need heating his blood.

"Someday?" she asked, her voice a little crestfallen.

He arched a brow. "Sooner?"

"Yes," she said, hope bleeding back in.

He tilted his head and studied her for a long moment. "Now?"

"Yes, Sir. Please." Her eyes were so wide and earnest that if he hadn't loved her before, he would've fallen just then.

He hardened in an instant, for the first time in his life feeling his mind, body, and heart align with one need, one purpose. Claiming this woman. Forever. In any and every way. "Undress and present yourself, Mia."

Staring into his eyes, she slowly unzipped her dress. That was all it took to bare her body to his gaze. She folded it, then placed it on the corner of his bed. Next, she removed her shoes. And then Mia knelt on the floor, knees wide, palms up on her thighs, back straight, head down. Beautiful.

Kyler pulled the necklace from the box and unlocked it. "I give this to you to wear tonight with the understanding that we need to discuss what it means to both of us, what the rules and expectations will be between us, and who we are going to be as a couple. Do you agree?"

"Yes, Sir," she said, her voice reverent. And it slayed him, it really did. Because this meant as much to her as it did to him. Everything.

"But for tonight, I will just ask, will you be mine, Mia Breslin? Body, heart, and soul? Look at me."

She did, and her eyes were bright with tears. "Yes, Sir. I promise. Body, heart, and soul."

"And I promise, in return, that I will be just as fully yours. Will you wear my collar?" His body was strung tight in anticipation of seeing it on her.

"Yes, Sir. It would be an honor."

He held it down in front of her mouth, and without him having to ask, Mia leaned forward and pressed her lips to the heart. The beauty of her submission nearly took him to his knees.

Kyler came behind her and draped the choker around her neck, and then he clicked it shut. He didn't lock it, not tonight, because that was a layer of commitment he wanted to save for when they'd worked everything out. But knowing the chain was unlocked took absolutely nothing away from seeing her wear his collar. He turned the chain so that the diamond heart hung just below the hollow of her throat. Standing in front of her, emotion made his chest feel too small to contain his heart. How had he gotten so lucky? Because he never thought he'd shed his solitude, let alone find love. Love with an amazing woman who accepted him, mistakes and fuck-ups and all.

"Beautiful Mia," he said. He took her hands and helped her rise. And then he got undressed too, until they were naked standing before one another. Naked except for her collar and the new bandage over his ribs, the parts of themselves they'd given to each other. "Sleep with me? I want you in my arms."

They crawled into bed together, her back pressed to his front, their legs intertwined. His cock was hard and arousal flooded through him, but Kyler just wanted to hold her in this perfect moment of calm and peace and belonging.

He thought sleeping with someone else might be odd or hard to adjust to. But her warmth and her touch lulled him and relaxed him in a way he'd never before experienced. He just hoped to God this wasn't all a dream. He just hoped that Mia was his. For keeps.

* * * *

Sunlight against her eyelids woke Mia slowly, but the moment the fog of sleep lifted from her brain, she gasped.

"Hey, hey, it's okay," Kyler said, leaning up on an elbow behind her, his fingers stroking over her collar. "I've got you."

"Did last night really happen?" she asked, absolutely awed at how Kyler had put himself out there, at the words he'd given her, at the cool weight of his collar around her neck. Last night had given her some of the best moments of her entire life.

"It did." He kissed her shoulder. Her neck. Her ear. His kisses awakened other parts of her body, too. "You still own me completely."

"God, Kyler. I feel the same way." She looked up at him, and he claimed her mouth. His hand held her face, his cock swelling against her ass. She ground back against him, need flooding her body.

He rocked against her. "Do you need me, baby?" His hand stroked down her body and pushed her top thigh back over his legs, opening her core to his touch. "Do you need me the way I need you?"

"Yes," she moaned as his hand slipped into the slickness between her lips.

"Feel that pussy, Mia. So wet. Is all this for me?" He pushed a finger deep inside her.

"All for you, Master," she said.

Kyler groaned. "That sounds so fucking good. I want you to scream it when you come," he said. His bottom arm slid under her neck and caught her in a chokehold, while he pushed a second finger inside her and fucked her with his hand, the pads of his fingers stroking her G-spot and making her wetter and wetter. "Play with your clit, Mia."

Mia's fingers fell into the wetness Kyler was drawing out from her. She pressed hard circles over her clit and moaned at the overload of sensation. His grip tightened around her throat, and she rasped in a breath, loving the burn. Need and affection coiled hard and fast inside her, settling between her legs and threatening to explode her apart into a million pieces. "Oh, fuck," she whispered.

"What are you going to say when you come?" he gritted out.

"All...for...you, Master," she managed, her voice strained by the way his arm squeezed her throat. "All for you, Master." He fucked her harder with his hand, his fingers stroking and stroking that dizzying place inside her until she felt an urgent outward pressure building, building. "All for you, Master," she said again, her voice barely audible. He added a third finger and curled them inside her. Mia unleashed a strangled, strained scream, *"AllforyouMaster!"*

Her whole body bowed on the orgasm and her pussy clenched so hard that her come ran onto her thigh and slid between her cheeks. Her body thrashed and twitched, the release going on and on before finally ebbing away.

"Jesus Christ," Kyler said, shoving her knees up and her shoulders forward, pushing her into a ball. "Have to get inside you."

And then his tip was right there and sliding deep.

He froze. "Fuck. Condom."

Her hand grabbed his hip, hard. "Don't leave me," she said. "We're both clean. I'm on birth control. Don't leave me."

"You want my come inside you, baby?" His voice was gritty and so full of sex it made her pussy fist his cock in an aftershock of her orgasm.

"Want all of you, Master. Please."

"Then you'll have me," he said, gripping her hip and driving balls deep. They both shouted, and then Kyler was drilling into her, going deeper than any man ever had before, his cock filling her pussy, his hand sliding up to her throat, his collar circling her neck. Nothing could be better than this.

He rolled them so that he was on top, his weight pressing her stomach into the mattress. "I want all of you, too," he growled. Shifting up, his right hand still gripping her throat, the thumb of his other hand lightly caressed her anus. "I want this, Mia." He sucked noisily for a second, and then his wet thumb pressed against her back hole, pushed in a little, and then a little more.

Mia groaned and arched her back, the invasion making her hotter even though it was uncomfortable.

"That's a tight fucking asshole." He pushed his thumb deeper, his thick knuckle popping past the ring of muscle. He fucked her ass in shallow strokes until he could work his finger deeper, until he was in up to his second knuckle. It burned so brightly, so painfully, so good, and made her feel fuller than she'd ever been in her life. "We'll have to talk about double penetration, won't we?" His breath was hot and urgent in her ear. "About all the ways we might be able to fulfill your fantasies. Every single one."

"Oh, Kyler," she rasped, overwhelmed by his actions and his words and everything she felt for him.

"Gonna spend every day driving you wild, Mia. Making you come and scream my name." His thumb and his cock both sank deep.

Mia screamed in pleasure. Suddenly, being filled in both holes was too much, not enough, everything. She came in an unexpected burst of sensation, her body writhing beneath him as she moaned.

"Yes, Mia. Yes." He gripped her by the back of her neck and slammed his cock into her pussy, once again alternating his strokes with those of his thumb in her ass. She wanted more there, but it overwhelmed her, too. "Arch your back and hold your cheeks spread."

Mia shifted on a groan, his cock battering her G-spot every time he bottomed out now, his thumb moving faster. Without warning, he withdrew from her ass. Mia shouted and arched harder, and then his weight came down on her, his body covering hers.

"Come again, baby. Come again," he gritted out, one hand fisting in her hair, the other gripping the front of her throat. Hard.

That was all it took. "Master," she cried, her whole body shuddering as her core spasmed, the release smaller this time, but she was so sensitive that it felt every bit as intense.

When her body calmed, Kyler eased out of her and rolled her onto her back. And then he settled between her thighs, his length easily sliding deep. He cradled her head in his hands, his cock moving inside her slow and easy as he looked deep into her eyes.

"My sweet girl," he said, his expression intense, his body trembling, an edge to his tone despite the tenderness of his words.

"Me and you," she said, squeezing her legs around him. "I love you, Kyler."

His face crumpled as his whole body went taut. His mouth dropped open on a silent shout, and then he was coming and groaning and fucking her in a series of punctuated thrusts. It was one of the sexiest things she'd ever seen, the face of a big, strong man, falling apart. Because of her.

Their bodies calming, Kyler stroked his hand over her hair. "You're the best thing that ever happened to me, Mia. Hands down. My whole life."

She couldn't help the wetness at the corners of her eyes. She'd never heard words spoken with more conviction. "Yeah? Well, then I hope this blissful, perfect moment is the worst one we ever have."

"Amen to that," he said, smiling. And then his expression grew serious. "I'm not always an easy man, and I know that. And I'm going to make mistakes. Sometimes, I'll probably be fucking hard to serve."

She chuckled. "Don't worry. I'll be a brat just to even us out."

He grinned. And then he stroked his fingers over his collar where it laid around her neck. "But I also promise to take care of you and to love you and to always be true. The rest we'll figure out together."

"I promise that, too," she said. As she stared into Kyler's eyes, Mia was so grateful that she'd taken a chance and gone to Blasphemy that night all those weeks ago because for the first time in her life, there wasn't a single thing more she wanted. She'd taken a chance at living deliberately, living deeply, and sucking out all the marrow of life, just like Dani said. And it had brought Mia more than she'd ever hoped.

It had brought her everything.

Everything in the form of a good man promising her his body, his heart, and his soul, and committed to taking care of hers in return. It seemed to Mia that if you had that kind of partner, that kind of companion, and that kind of love in life, you had it all.

* * * *

Also from 1001 Dark Nights and Laura Kaye, discover Hard As Steel.

Sign up for the 1001 Dark Nights Newsletter
and be entered to win a Tiffany Key necklace.

There's a contest every month!

Go to www.1001DarkNights.com to subscribe.

As a bonus, all subscribers will receive a free
1001 Dark Nights story
The First Night
by Lexi Blake & M.J. Rose

Turn the page for a full list of the
1001 Dark Nights fabulous novellas...

Discover 1001 Dark Nights Collection Three

HIDDEN INK by Carrie Ann Ryan
A Montgomery Ink Novella

BLOOD ON THE BAYOU by Heather Graham
A Cafferty & Quinn Novella

SEARCHING FOR MINE by Jennifer Probst
A Searching For Novella

DANCE OF DESIRE by Christopher Rice

ROUGH RHYTHM by Tessa Bailey
A Made In Jersey Novella

DEVOTED by Lexi Blake
A Masters and Mercenaries Novella

Z by Larissa Ione
A Demonica Underworld Novella

FALLING UNDER YOU by Laurelin Paige
A Fixed Trilogy Novella

EASY FOR KEEPS by Kristen Proby
A Boudreaux Novella

UNCHAINED by Elisabeth Naughton
An Eternal Guardians Novella

HARD TO SERVE by Laura Kaye
A Hard Ink Novella

DRAGON FEVER by Donna Grant
A Dark Kings Novella

KAYDEN/SIMON by Alexandra Ivy/Laura Wright
A Bayou Heat Novella

STRUNG UP by Lorelei James
A Blacktop Cowboys® Novella

MIDNIGHT UNTAMED by Lara Adrian
A Midnight Breed Novella

TRICKED by Rebecca Zanetti
A Dark Protectors Novella

DIRTY WICKED by Shayla Black
A Wicked Lovers Novella

A SEDUCTIVE INVITATION by Lauren Blakely
A Seductive Nights New York Novella

SWEET SURRENDER by Liliana Hart
A MacKenzie Family Novella

For more information, visit www.1001DarkNights.com.

Discover 1001 Dark Nights Collection One

FOREVER WICKED by Shayla Black
CRIMSON TWILIGHT by Heather Graham
CAPTURED IN SURRENDER by Liliana Hart
SILENT BITE: A SCANGUARDS WEDDING by Tina Folsom
DUNGEON GAMES by Lexi Blake
AZAGOTH by Larissa Ione
NEED YOU NOW by Lisa Renee Jones
SHOW ME, BABY by Cherise Sinclair
ROPED IN by Lorelei James
TEMPTED BY MIDNIGHT by Lara Adrian
THE FLAME by Christopher Rice
CARESS OF DARKNESS by Julie Kenner

Also from 1001 Dark Nights

TAME ME by J. Kenner

For more information, visit www.1001DarkNights.com.

Discover 1001 Dark Nights Collection Two

WICKED WOLF by Carrie Ann Ryan
WHEN IRISH EYES ARE HAUNTING by Heather Graham
EASY WITH YOU by Kristen Proby
MASTER OF FREEDOM by Cherise Sinclair
CARESS OF PLEASURE by Julie Kenner
ADORED by Lexi Blake
HADES by Larissa Ione
RAVAGED by Elisabeth Naughton
DREAM OF YOU by Jennifer L. Armentrout
STRIPPED DOWN by Lorelei James
RAGE/KILLIAN by Alexandra Ivy/Laura Wright
DRAGON KING by Donna Grant
PURE WICKED by Shayla Black
HARD AS STEEL by Laura Kaye
STROKE OF MIDNIGHT by Lara Adrian
ALL HALLOWS EVE by Heather Graham
KISS THE FLAME by Christopher Rice
DARING HER LOVE by Melissa Foster
TEASED by Rebecca Zanetti
THE PROMISE OF SURRENDER by Liliana Hart

Also from 1001 Dark Nights

THE SURRENDER GATE By Christopher Rice
SERVICING THE TARGET By Cherise Sinclair

For more information, visit www.1001DarkNights.com.

About Laura Kaye

Laura is the *New York Times* and *USA Today* bestselling author of over twenty books in contemporary and paranormal romance and romantic suspense. Laura's Hard Ink series has won many awards, including the RT Reviewers' Choice Award for Best Romance Suspense of 2014 for *Hard As You Can*. Her upcoming Raven Riders series debuts in April 2016. Growing up, Laura's large extended family believed in the supernatural, and family lore involving angels, ghosts, and evil-eye curses cemented in Laura a life-long fascination with storytelling and all things paranormal. She lives in Maryland with her husband, two daughters, and cute-but-bad dog, and appreciates her view of the Chesapeake Bay every day. Learn more at www.LauraKayeAuthor.com.

Blasphemy

Announcing a New Erotic Romance Series from Laura Kaye…

From the ruins of an abandoned church comes Baltimore's hottest and most exclusive BDSM club. Twelve Masters. Infinite fantasies. Welcome to Blasphemy…

Bound to Submit
Coming September 13, 2016

He thinks he caused her pain, but she knows he's the only one who can heal her…

Kenna Sloane lost her career and her arm in the Marines, and now she feels like she's losing herself. Submission is the only thing that ever freed her from pain and made her feel secure, and Kenna needs to serve again. Bad. The only problem is the Dom she wants once refused her submission and broke her heart, but, scarred on the inside and out, she's not looking for love this time. She's not even sure she's capable.

Griffin Hudson is haunted by the mistakes that cost him the only woman he ever loved. Now she's back at his BDSM club, Blasphemy, and more beautiful than ever, and she's asking for his help with the pain he knows he caused. Even though he's scared to hurt her again, he can't refuse her, because he'd give anything to earn a second chance. And this time, he'll hold on forever.

Ride Hard

Raven Riders #1
By Laura Kaye
Now Available!

Brotherhood. Club. Family.
They live and ride by their own rules.
These are the Raven Riders...

Raven Riders Motorcycle Club President Dare Kenyon rides hard and values loyalty above all else. He'll do anything to protect the brotherhood of bikers—the only family he's got—as well as those who can't defend themselves. So when mistrustful Haven Randall lands on the club's doorstep scared that she's being hunted, Dare takes her in, swears to keep her safe, and pushes to learn the secrets overshadowing her pretty smile.

Haven fled from years of abuse at the hands of her criminal father and is suspicious of any man's promises, including those of the darkly sexy and overwhelmingly intense Ravens' leader. But as the powerful attraction between them flares to life, Dare pushes her boundaries and tempts her to want things she never thought she could.

The past never dies without a fight, but Dare Kenyon's never backed down before...

* * * *

"So much better out here," Haven said, the night air cool against the tingling warmth of her skin. Although she was pretty sure that not all of the heat burning through her insides was from the alcohol—her unusual flirtatiousness and closeness to Dare over the past half hour had made her desperate with a heat that had nothing to do with her drinking game.

She walked to the railing and leaned against it, chuckling a little at herself for needing the support it offered. She felt so damn free, and it was a heady, exhilarating thing.

"What's funny?" Dare asked, settling a hip against the railing right beside her. Arms crossed, jaw ticking with tension, dark eyes blazing, he was staring at her like he wanted to reprimand her or devour her. Oddly, neither alarmed her the way she would've expected it to.

Haven shook her head, leaning it back and letting her gaze float over the night sky. Blurry points of light swam in the moonlit heavens. It was beautiful and peaceful despite the pounding bass beat of music thumping from inside the clubhouse. "Not funny, just good. Happy, you know? Being able to do something a little... scary, but knowing I'd be safe doing it." When Dare's gaze narrowed, she shrugged. "I don't know."

A long moment passed before Dare finally spoke. "You are safe here, Haven. Never doubt it."

Peering up at him, she nodded, all kinds of words sitting on the tip of her tongue, challenging her to let them fly. "It's weird feeling safe— or at least safer—after a lifetime of not. It makes me want to try things I could never let myself try before. It makes me..." She shook her head and dipped her chin.

Dare stepped closer, his thighs coming up against her hip. He lifted her chin and made her look at him. The contact combined with the command in the gesture lanced white-hot desire through her veins. "Makes you what?"

"Want to feel alive," she whispered, her heart suddenly racing in her chest.

Dare's jaw ticked again as his gaze swept over her face. She didn't think she was imagining the raw emotion pouring off of him and wrapping around her, but she wasn't sure if she was reading that emotion right or projecting her own desire onto him.

"Do you feel alive, Dare?" she asked, the alcohol flowing through her and the night spinning around her like she was walking through a dream.

"Jesus," he bit out.

The rough desperation in his voice made her wet between her legs. "Just once," she whispered, not sure what she was asking him for.

But he seemed to know. Because his hand was suddenly tangled in her hair and his mouth was suddenly on hers, claiming, probing, tasting. Haven moaned and parted her lips, inviting him deeper.

Dare jerked back from her, his fingers rubbing roughly over his lips. "Fuck, I'm sorry."

On instinct, Haven's body pursued his, pinning his back to the railing. "Please don't stop," she said as her hands gripped his shoulders. She had the strongest urge to climb him, to wrap her legs around him, to grind against the hard bulge pressing electrically against her belly.

"Please," she whispered, tilting her mouth toward his. "I liked it."

Dare's hand cupped the back of her head. "You're killing me."

"Dare," she said, her body restless against his.

In a move that sent the world spinning, he flipped them around so that she was the one pinned against the railing. He pushed his legs between hers and leaned down over her, forcing her to arch her back, to yield, to open to him. "Tell me what you want from me. Say the words," he said, his eyes absolutely on fire.

Her heart was a runaway train in her chest, frantic and picking up speed. The thought of giving voice to her desires was terrifying and thrilling and dizzying all at once.

"I want your mouth," she said. The words sounded odder out loud than they had in her head, but they were more accurate than asking him to kiss her—because her mouth wasn't the only place she wanted his.

"Jesus," he rasped again, his mouth coming down on hers once more.

The whimper she released was part relief, part anticipation. It had been so long since she'd kissed someone that she felt a little uncertain, but Dare's intensity barely allowed her the capacity to worry about it. He was like a dark storm bearing down on her, relentless, magnetic, all-consuming.

Rough callouses from his hands scratched against her cheeks as he guided her. Hard breaths spilled over her lips, and the wet slide of his tongue tasted like whiskey and desire and man. Her hands found the soft length of his hair, and her breasts pushed against the hard plane of his chest.

Then her lips were freed as his mouth slid over her skin—exploring her cheek, her jaw, her ear, her neck. He hiked her up to sit on the wide railing, the move surprising a gasp out of her, especially as he crowded the space between her legs, pushing himself closer, bringing his erection against the place between her legs craving friction, hardness, so much more of him. Maybe even all of him.

One strong arm wrapped around her back and held her steady, while the other hand stroked her hair, her face, her breast. The soft groans and breathy grunts spilling out of him were delicious and thrilling, and bolstered her confidence that she wasn't the only one losing herself in this moment, in these touches. She almost couldn't believe this was happening, and part of her was certain she must be dreaming. Because Haven Randall didn't have beautiful things in her life. At least, never before.

Discover More Laura Kaye

Hard As Steel
A Hard Ink/Raven Riders Crossover

After identifying her employer's dangerous enemies, Jessica Jakes takes refuge at the compound of the Raven Riders Motorcycle Club. Fellow Hard Ink tattooist and Raven leader Ike Young promises to keep Jess safe for as long as it takes, which would be perfect if his close, personal, round-the-clock protection didn't make it so hard to hide just how much she wants him--and always has.

Ike Young loved and lost a woman in trouble once before. The last thing he needs is alone time with the sexiest and feistiest woman he's ever known, one he's purposely kept at a distance for years. Now, Ike's not sure he can keep his hands or his heart to himself--or that he even wants to anymore. And that means he has to do whatever it takes to hold on to Jess forever.

On behalf of 1001 Dark Nights,

Liz Berry and M.J. Rose would like to thank ~

Steve Berry
Doug Scofield
Kim Guidroz
Jillian Stein
InkSlinger PR
Dan Slater
Asha Hossain
Chris Graham
Pamela Jamison
Jessica Johns
Dylan Stockton
Richard Blake
BookTrib After Dark
The Dinner Party Show
and Simon Lipskar

40572620R00094

Made in the USA
San Bernardino, CA
22 October 2016